BLAME IT ON THE BIKINI
OCEAN SHORES #4

BARBARA FREETHY

Fog City Publishing

PRAISE FOR BARBARA FREETHY

"A fabulous, page-turning combination of romance and intrigue. Fans of Nora Roberts and Elizabeth Lowell will love this book." — *NYT Bestselling Author Kristin Hannah on Golden Lies*

"Freethy has a gift for creating complex, appealing characters and emotionally involving, often suspenseful, sometimes magical stories." — *Library Journal on Suddenly One Summer*

"Barbara Freethy is a master storyteller with a gift for spinning tales about ordinary people in extraordinary situations and drawing readers into their lives." — *Romance Reviews Today*

"Freethy is at the top of her form. Fans of Nora Roberts will find a similar tone here, framed in Freethy's own spare, elegant style." — *Contra Costa Times on Summer Secrets*

"The story grabbed me immediately and made me fall in love with it. The characters were well-developed and multi-faceted, not only the two main characters but all the minor ones as well. The Ocean Shores community is where I would like to live!" *Bonnie – Goodreads on Hopelessly Romantic*

"Barbara Freethy is a master storyteller!" *Romance Reviews Today*

"Freethy hits the ground running as she kicks off another winning romantic suspense series...Freethy is at her prime with a superb combo of engaging characters and gripping plot." — *Publishers' Weekly on Silent Run*

PRAISE FOR BARBARA FREETHY

"This story was so much fun to read. The characters are quirky yet strong willed. The setting is idyllic. And the plot line was laugh-out-loud fun. I'm looking forward to following along as each tenant gets his/her own happy ending, especially the wounded warrior who's keeping to himself while he heals." *Robin – Goodreads on Hopelessly Romantic*

"Freethy's zesty storytelling will keep readers hooked, and the sisters' loving but prickly interactions will make anyone with a sibling smile." *Publishers Weekly on Summer Secrets*

"Gifted author Barbara Freethy creates an irresistible tale of family secrets, riveting adventure and heart-touching romance." *NYT Bestselling Author Susan Wiggs on Summer Secrets*

"Freethy skillfully keeps the reader on the hook , and her tantalizing and believable tale has it all -- romance, adventure and mystery." *Booklist (Starred Review) on Summer Secrets*

"A warm, moving story of the power of love." *NYT Bestselling Author Debbie Macomber on Daniel's Gift*

"Freethy has a gift for creating complex, appealing characters and emotionally involving, often suspenseful, sometimes magical stories." — *Library Journal on Suddenly One Summer*

"I have just finished CAN'T FIGHT THE MOONLIGHT and WOW such an emotional story. Absolutely loved this book...and can't wait for the next one!" *Booklovers Anonymous*

ALSO BY BARBARA FREETHY

Ocean Shores Series

Hopelessly Romantic

Summer Loving

Moonlight Feels Right

Blame It On The Bikini

Love Me Like You Do

Whisper Lake Series

Always With Me

My Wildest Dream

Can't Fight The Moonlight

Just One Kiss

If We Never Met

Tangled Up In You

Next Time I Fall

For a complete list of books, visit my website!

CHAPTER ONE

Grayson Holt's jaw tightened in frustration as his father's voice crackled through the car speaker.

"It's just one month, Gray. Four weeks. That's all I'm asking," Emerson Holt said.

"Four weeks is a ridiculous waste of time," he replied, navigating his Audi along the Pacific Coast Highway, the ocean stretching endlessly to his right. The GPS indicated he was five minutes from Oceanside—five minutes from an obligation he'd been trying to avoid for months. But he'd run out of time and options. "The financial analysis is crystal clear. This building is an underperforming asset we should have divested years ago, Dad. You know that."

"What I know is that there's more to Ocean Shores than numbers on a spreadsheet."

"Actually, there isn't." Grayson fought to keep his voice level despite his rising anger. "The property values in this area have skyrocketed. We're sitting on prime beachfront real estate that's generating a fraction of its potential return. We could sell it tomorrow and make a substantial profit."

His father's sigh was heavy with disappointment. "You're

thirty-three years old, Grayson, and you still think everything can be reduced to profit margins."

"That's literally the point of our business." He glanced in the rearview mirror before changing lanes. "Holt Enterprises isn't a charity. We acquire properties, optimize their value, and sell when the market conditions are favorable. You know this."

"And yet I've held onto Ocean Shores for thirty-five years."

"Which has never made sense to me."

A moment of silence followed, and Grayson could picture his father in his expansive corner office in downtown Los Angeles, staring out at the skyline, gathering his thoughts.

"That's why you need to stay there," Emerson finally said. "You need to understand why some investments are worth more than their market value."

"I don't have time for this. I have quarterly projections due next week, the Singapore acquisition is at a critical stage, and the board meeting—"

"The company won't collapse without you for a month. Our team is more than capable."

"But—"

"This isn't negotiable, Gray." His father's voice took on the steely edge that had intimidated countless business associates over the decades. "You want my approval to sell Ocean Shores? Fine. But I'm not signing off until you've lived there for one month. Helen has set everything up for you. Your apartment has been furnished, and the refrigerator and cupboards stocked with essentials. You'll have everything you need."

"That's not the point."

"The point," his father said firmly, "is that you need to experience Ocean Shores for yourself. Meet the residents. See what we'd be taking from them if we sell."

"We'd be giving them a generous relocation package."

"Money isn't everything, son."

Grayson nearly laughed at the irony of those words coming from Emerson Holt, a man whose singular focus on wealth acquisition had built a billion-dollar real-estate empire. "That's rich, coming from you."

"Perhaps I've learned a few things over the years. Things I'd like to spare you from learning the hard way."

An uncomfortable knot settled in his stomach. His dad's words were more emotionally weighted than most of their conversations, and he didn't know what to make of them.

"One month at the beach," his father continued. "Not the roughest assignment you've ever been given. You might enjoy yourself."

"One month. The second it's over, we're listing the property."

"We'll see."

The call ended, and Grayson continued down the highway for another few miles, his mind far away from the endless blue sea. He had so many more things he'd rather be doing than this, but it was four weeks. He just had to get through it, and then he would never have to think about Ocean Shores again.

A few moments later, he pulled into the parking lot behind the two-story building and turned off the engine. He sat for a moment, staring at the structure in front of him. He'd made a brief visit here in September, seven months ago, and doubted much had changed. The sign at the parking lot entrance looked freshly painted, and the newly landscaped hedges and flower beds added to the neat appearance, but there was no denying the eighteen-unit apartment building had been built fifty years ago and was showing its age.

He grabbed his leather briefcase from the passenger seat and got out of the car, immediately assaulted by the pungent scent of salt air and the distant rhythm of waves. It was a warm, sunny Friday evening with the temperature still in the low eighties. He decided to leave his bags in the car until he located his apartment. Then he'd get settled in.

As he made his way toward the entrance, he started sweating. He was definitely overdressed in his suit and tie, his Italian loafers crunching on the gravel as he approached the building. The courtyard entrance was unassuming—a simple gate with a small plaque bearing the Ocean Shores name. Grayson pushed it open and stepped into what felt like another world.

The interior courtyard was alive with activity. A sparkling pool occupied the center of the space, surrounded by residents lounging on chairs. Laughter drifted from a group gathered around a barbecue area, where a man was flipping burgers while telling an animated story. At another table, two women were engaged in what appeared to be an intense card game, slapping down cards with dramatic flair.

Potted plants and string lights created an atmosphere of casual charm. The building formed a rectangular shape, with all doors facing the courtyard, creating an odd sense of intimacy. The coming and going of every resident would be visible to anyone in the common area, and that lack of privacy was not appealing to him, but no one in the courtyard appeared irritated; they looked happy.

As his gaze swept the area, he found some of the faces to be familiar from his brief visit months ago, although he couldn't remember many of their names.

Then he saw *her*, the beautiful and irritating Lexie Price, the manager's niece, the woman determined to convince him he shouldn't sell the building. She was the one person he hadn't forgotten.

As she emerged from the pool, her dark hair was slicked back from her face, highlighting her striking features—high cheekbones, full lips, and brown eyes that had challenged him the moment they'd met. But it was the hot pink bikini that temporarily short-circuited his thought process, revealing stunning curves he hadn't fully appreciated during their previous encounter.

He quickly looked down at his phone as it vibrated with a message, grateful for the distraction. But the business text couldn't prevent him from looking up again, looking for her…

Unfortunately, his view was blocked by a colorful beach ball hurtling directly at his face. He jerked back, but he was too late. The ball connected with his forehead, throwing him off-balance. His arms windmilled as he teetered on the pool's edge.

For one suspended moment, he thought he might regain his balance. Then gravity won, and he plunged into the water with a splash.

The shock of cold water enveloped him as he sank, his expensive suit immediately waterlogged. He surfaced, gasping and sputtering, to find the entire courtyard had fallen silent, all eyes fixed on him. Before he could haul himself out, he saw Lexie standing at the pool's edge, a mixture of surprise and amusement playing across her face.

"Well," she said, extending a hand to him, "you certainly arrived with a splash."

Nervous laughter rippled through the gathered residents. Grayson ignored her outstretched hand and pulled himself out of the pool, water cascading from his ruined suit.

"I'm so sorry!" A young boy ran up to him with a worried expression on his face. "I didn't mean to hit you."

"It's fine," Grayson managed, noting that the boy couldn't have been more than six or seven.

"I told you to be careful, Henry," a woman said, putting her arm around the boy's shoulders. Then she gave him a wary look. "I'm Paige Kendry, Henry's mother. "If you need to have that suit dry-cleaned or maybe get a new one, I can pay for it."

"Don't worry about it," he muttered, suddenly realizing he'd lost his phone. As he turned his head, he saw it at the bottom of the pool. "Damn. My phone."

"I'll get it," Lexie said, immediately going back into the pool to retrieve his phone.

He frowned as she came back to the surface and moved up the steps to hand it to him. His phone was definitely not designed for submersion in a swimming pool. "This is done."

"I'm sorry."

"It's fine. I'm going to find my apartment."

"You're in 11B, at the top of the stairs in the corner," she added, tipping her head to the right. "You have keys, right? We sent them to someone named Helen."

"I have them." He picked up his briefcase, which he'd thankfully managed to drop on the ground before landing in the pool, and made his way toward the stairs, very aware of the attention he was drawing. He was dripping wet, and his shoes squelched with every step, offering a wonderfully humiliating soundtrack to his arrival.

When he got upstairs, he was happy to put the key in the door and step into his apartment, away from those far-too-interested eyes.

The apartment was modern in décor, with designer touches added to the gray couch and matching chairs, the glass coffee table, and the cabinet containing the television. A white dining room table with four chairs sat adjacent to the kitchen, which gleamed with shiny stainless-steel appliances.

Before he could make his way into the bedroom, a knock sounded at his door.

He opened it to find Lexie with a towel wrapped around her hips and a phone in her hands. "In case you need to make some calls before you can get another phone, you can use mine."

"That's not necessary. I can text from my computer until I get another phone."

"Are you sure?"

"Positive."

"Okay. If you change your mind, I'm downstairs in 2A, right next to Josie's apartment." She paused. "I don't know why you decided to stay here for a few weeks, but I hope you'll take the time to get to know the tenants, to understand that we have a community here. This might be a simple business decision for you, but for us, it's our home."

"I'm aware of your feelings on that matter," he said, noting the anger flaring in her pretty brown eyes. She really was a strikingly beautiful woman, even with wet hair and not a speck of makeup on her face.

"But you don't care about feelings," she said with annoyance.

"Look, I'm not trying to hurt anyone. If we decide to sell, there will be generous relocation packages for the tenants."

"Because money fixes everything, right?"

"Not everything, but it can fix a lot."

"From my experience, it can also ruin people. But, clearly, I'm not going to change your mind tonight." She paused. "We're having a barbecue in the courtyard. Why don't you join us after you dry off and get settled in?"

"I have work to do, and I had a late lunch. I'm going to be here for a month. There will be plenty of time for me to meet people."

"Fine," she said with exasperation. "But since half the building is in the courtyard, you're missing a great opportunity."

As she left the apartment, he let out a sigh, feeling completely off his game. He'd wanted to arrive as the professional business owner he was, not some idiot who fell into the swimming pool. That incident had changed the power dynamic, and he needed to get it back. But first, he needed to get his suitcases out of his car and take a shower.

Heading down the stairs, he was once again greeted by the sound of conversation and laughter. He tried not to make eye contact with anyone, moving quickly into the parking lot. Once at the car, he grabbed his suitcases and headed back inside. The little boy who'd hit him with the ball and his mother, Paige, were standing by the stairs, clearly waiting for him.

The little boy held a piece of paper in his hand. "This is for you."

"Henry wrote you a note," Paige added.

"That wasn't necessary," he said as he looked down at the note where Henry had written *I'm sorry* in big colorful, uneven letters. "Thank you for this. I accept your apology."

"I hate that your first impression of us was getting hit in the head by a ball," Paige said. "I know you're here to assess the building and our community."

He frowned at the worry in her expression. "Like I said, it was not a big deal. But I would like to change. So, if you'll excuse me..."

"Of course. I hope you'll join us for dinner or a drink later, once you get settled in."

"I'll see," he said, not wanting to get into a longer conversation.

As Paige and Henry left, he saw Lexie and several other people watching him, their expressions a mix of suspicion and worry. He quickly turned and jogged up the stairs. He needed to get himself together before he had any further discussions with the tenants. Once he changed, he hoped he'd start feeling more like himself.

Lexie gave Paige and Henry a smile as they returned to the pool area. "That was nice of you to give him a note."

"I'm not sure it helped," Paige replied. "I don't think he's coming to the barbecue. I'm so sorry this happened, Lexie."

"It's fine," she assured her. "We have plenty of time to make Grayson Holt see how great this place is and how amazing we are." She tried to infuse confidence into her voice, not wanting to let anyone get discouraged too early.

"Can I play with Olivia?" Henry asked.

"Sure," Paige said, following her son to the other side of the pool, where Olivia was playing with a boat on the steps of the pool, her mother, Bree, watching over her.

"I'm not sure forever would be enough time for that man to see how great this place is," Kaia said with a pragmatic shrug of her shoulders.

Kaia Mercer, a pretty redheaded paramedic who dealt with life and death situations, was also the most cynical person in their group of friends and tenants. And she always spoke the truth as she saw it, with little to no sugarcoating. Before she could reply, her aunt, Josie, joined them.

"It's enough time," Josie said with a bright smile.

At sixty-five, her aunt had an optimistic vibrancy that made her seem years younger. She'd been the manager at Ocean Shores for thirty-five years and had become a second mom to the younger residents and a good friend to the older tenants.

Lexie couldn't imagine what her aunt would do if the building was sold. It was her home, her career—her everything—which made her aunt's cheerful attitude even more inexplicable. Josie never seemed to be that worried about losing the building. She didn't know if that was just because her aunt had decided not to think about things that bothered her or just didn't understand the gravity of their current situation.

Giving her aunt a doubtful look, she said, "I don't get it, Aunt Josie. Why are you so hopeful?"

"Because we have him for a month. We just need to show Grayson how charming, supportive, and caring our community is. Make him feel like family."

"I don't think he wants to be a part of our family," she said. "And his stay certainly didn't start out well with his fall into the pool and the destruction of his very expensive phone."

Josie gave a dismissive, uncaring wave. "That was an accident. I'm sure he won't hold it against us."

"I wouldn't be certain of that. I invited him to join the barbecue, and he said no. And Henry's apology letter didn't make a difference. He's clearly here under duress."

"Why do you think his father made him come here for a month, Josie?" Kaia asked curiously.

Her aunt gave them a somewhat secretive smile. "Grayson's father, Emerson Holt, is a fair man and a smart one, too. If he thinks Grayson can make a better decision after a month with us, then I have to believe it's a possibility."

"If Emerson doesn't want to sell, why did he give the control of this property to his son?" she asked, still feeling like her aunt wasn't being completely forthcoming.

"I'm not sure. But time reveals all. Now, I'm going to get a burger. They smell delicious, don't they?"

As Josie moved toward the grill, Kaia gave her a pointed look. "Your aunt isn't telling us everything. And what was that about time reveals all? Has she been reading the Tarot cards again?"

"She's always doing that," she said with a smile. "But I agree that she's acting very strangely about this whole thing. She's usually open with me about everything. She's not a secretive person."

"Maybe you just think that because she's good at keeping secrets," Kaia said. "She was once an Oscar-winning actress, after all."

"That's true." In her twenties, her aunt had been an award-winning actress, but she'd given it all up after winning an Oscar and divorcing her husband of three years. The events had always seemed intertwined, but her aunt had never been forthcoming on that subject, either. "Secrets or no secrets, Aunt Josie might be right. We need to show Grayson Holt what a great community we have here and hope that will change his mind."

"Sure. A group of friendly people will definitely compete with the millions he could make on this property."

"Stop. I have enough doubts of my own. I don't need yours, too."

"Sorry," Kaia said. "I will do my part to be friendly."

"Thank you."

"I'm sure everyone else will, too, although I'm not sure about our newest tenant, the one who moved into Hunter's old apartment two weeks ago. What's his name again?"

"Jax Ridley. That's all I know. Aunt Josie said he was a friend of a friend, and when I quizzed her about him, she just said she thought he'd be a good fit."

"Maybe everyone who lives in that apartment is destined to

start out as a mystery man," Kaia said. "Hunter lived there for months before he started talking to any of us." She paused. "Speak of the devil..."

"You couldn't possibly be talking about me," Hunter said as he and Emmalyn McGuire joined them poolside, their hands intertwined, which always seemed to be the case these days. The past few months had seen their love story only get stronger, and seeing them together made her heart clench. Hunter had been a wounded warrior when he'd first moved into the building, but he'd found healing and love since then. Emmalyn had had to battle her share of demons, too, but now that they were together, they both seemed to be constantly smiling.

"I was just commenting that everyone who moved into your old apartment seems to have a little mystery behind them," Kaia said.

"Really?" Emmalyn asked curiously. "I haven't heard anything about the new tenant. What's the scoop, Lexie?"

She shrugged. "His name is Jax Ridley. That's all I know."

"Ridley is a good name for a riddle," Kaia said with a laugh. "I saw him from afar and gave him a wave. He acted like he didn't see me."

"Maybe he didn't see you," Hunter put in. "And maybe you need to give him a chance to settle in. This group can be a little overwhelming at first. Trust me, I know."

"But you came to love us," Lexie said. "Or at least one of us."

"I love all of you," he admitted, his smile broadening as he glanced at Emmalyn. "But one most of all."

"You're so sweet," Emmalyn said.

"And you two are too much," Kaia said dryly. "I need a drink to tamp down all this sugar."

As Kaia headed toward the bar that had been set up on a nearby table, Emmalyn said, "Is the new owner here? He's coming today, right?"

"He's here. But his entrance was a disaster. Henry hit him in the head with a beach ball, and he fell in the pool, with his phone in his hand."

"That sounds bad," Emmalyn said with worry in her eyes.

"It sounds kind of funny to me," Hunter said.

"Not funny," she said. "I tried to make nice. I offered to lend him my phone in case he needed to make some calls before he could replace his, but he threw that back in my face. I also invited him to the barbecue, and he said, 'No thanks.' But he's going to be here for a month, so hopefully we can get things back on track."

"A month is a good amount of time," Hunter said. "You don't have to win him over in one night."

"I guess," she said as Kaia rejoined them.

"I will say one thing about him," Kaia began. "He looked good wet. In fact, he's a very attractive man."

"Until he opens his mouth," she said dryly. "Then he sounds arrogant and entitled. I know his type. I worked with a bunch of them when I was a lawyer. He's the kind of man who thinks he's right about everything."

"We'll help him feel more comfortable here. Maybe I'll bake him some cookies."

"That worked for me," Hunter said with a laugh.

As Hunter and Emmalyn exchanged a kiss, she felt a little pang. She was more than a little happy to see her friend Emmalyn so in love. Finding that kind of connection wasn't easy. But she didn't have time to worry about love. She had one month to convince Grayson Holt not to sell Ocean Shores. It wouldn't be easy, but she wasn't going to let him take their home without a fight.

CHAPTER TWO

Lexie was still in fight mode Saturday morning, but she wasn't fighting with Grayson; she was fighting with her ten-year-old car. She'd tried several times to start it, hoping the sheer force of her will and her need to get to her job as a wedding photographer would somehow bring it back to life. But all she got was a click of finality every time she turned the key.

"No, no, no," she groaned, glancing at her watch. It was eight-thirty, and she needed to be at Seaside Cliff Resort at nine a.m. to start shooting the pre-wedding rituals at eleven a.m. "You cannot do this to me today," she told her car. That plea went unanswered, too.

Her battery had to be dead, and no doubt someone in the complex probably had jumper cables, but she didn't have time to hunt that down. She was already late.

Getting out of her car, she pulled up a rideshare app, sighing at the surge pricing. Even though it was early on a Saturday morning, clearly the universe had it in for her today.

She scrolled through her contacts—Kaia, Paige, Emmalyn... Voicemail, voicemail, voicemail. Everyone was probably asleep or already out, which included her aunt, who had gone with Margaret to the farmers' market.

Her phone vibrated with an incoming call, and she hoped it was one of her friends, but it was the bride's mother. She took a deep breath before answering. "Good morning, Mrs. Morrison."

"Lexie! Where are you?" The woman's voice was pitched high with stress. "The makeup artist is already here, and Tiffany is freaking out because one of her bridesmaids is stuck at the airport. I'm afraid Jordan might be getting cold feet because his best man says he was up all night and—"

"Mrs. Morrison," Lexie cut in with practiced calm, "everything will be fine. I'm on my way right now." A small lie, but a necessary one. "These pre-wedding jitters are completely normal."

"Everyone needs to see you're here so they'll calm down and—"

"I'll be there very soon. I'm not late. We're scheduled to start at nine. Just take a deep breath. Today will be beautiful."

As she ended the call, she caught sight of movement in her peripheral vision. Grayson Holt was walking toward his car, keys in hand, dressed in what appeared to be workout clothes—expensive ones, naturally. Even in workout clothes, the man couldn't help but exude wealth and privilege.

Before she could decide whether to swallow her pride and ask him for a ride, he glanced over, noticing her standing beside her open car door.

"Good morning," he said. "Is something wrong?"

"My car won't start. Dead battery, I think. Of all the days, it had to happen today."

"Are you heading somewhere important?"

"I'm photographing a wedding at Seaside Cliff Resort." She checked her watch again. "That I'm already late for."

"I can give you a jump if you have cables."

"I know there are some cables in the storage shed, but I don't have time to look, and none of my friends are around. I just need to call for a ride." She glanced down at her app again. "For some reason, the rideshare is very busy this morning."

Grayson hesitated, clearly working his way through an internal debate, then gave a resigned nod. "I can give you a ride. It's not too far from here, is it?"

"About fifteen minutes."

"Then grab your stuff, and let's go."

Relief coursed through her, immediately followed by discomfort at being indebted to him. But she had no choice. She grabbed her equipment and put it in the trunk of his Audi.

"Thank you," she said as she got into the passenger seat, immediately struck by the new-car smell and immaculate interior. It reminded her of her father's succession of luxury vehicles, each one replaced before it showed even a hint of wear. "I appreciate this."

He merely nodded and started the engine, which immediately purred to life. He didn't say anything as he put the resort into his GPS and then proceeded out of the parking lot.

After two minutes, the silence between them grew heavy. She wanted to break it, but she didn't know what to say. She couldn't get into an argument with him about the building while he was doing her a favor, and what else could they possibly discuss?

"So," he finally said, obviously deciding he was tired of the awkward silence, too, "Do you shoot a lot of weddings?"

"More than I would like. Nature and landscape photography is what I really love, but weddings provide a reliable income."

"Quite a departure from corporate law," he commented. "Didn't you tell me the last time I was here that you went to Georgetown? Weren't you working for your father's very prestigious law firm? It seems like you made quite a leap."

She could hear the implied criticism in his words. Clearly, he considered her jump a leap down, but that was okay. He wasn't the first to question her decisions. "I wanted to be able to work in a field where I could be creative and imaginative. I'm also no longer working eighty hours a week to make rich people richer. I call my own shots." She'd barely finished speaking when her phone rang. The bride this time. "I'm sorry. I have to take this. It's the bride."

"Go ahead."

"Hi, Tiffany! How are you feeling this morning?"

The bride's tearful voice spilled from the phone loud enough for Grayson to hear her. "Everything's falling apart, Lexie. The florist delivered the wrong centerpieces. Jordan hasn't texted me back in an hour. My mom is driving me crazy, and Kathleen is stuck at the airport. My wedding is turning into a disaster—"

"Take a deep breath," Lexie interrupted. "It's all going to work out. I'll be there shortly, and we're going to capture every beautiful moment of your day, starting with you getting ready with your bridesmaids. Remember how excited you were about those matching robes?"

"Yes," Tiffany said. "But what about Kathleen?"

"She'll make it. I'm sure Eileen has already sent a car for her," she said, referring to Tiffany's wedding planner, who had at times been happy to abdicate a lot of her responsibilities to Lexie. But, hopefully, she was working on getting Kathleen to the resort. If not, she'd deal with that when she arrived. "Why don't you and the other girls put on your robes and open that bottle of champagne your maid of honor brought? By the time you've had a glass, I'll be there, and we'll start creating the memories you'll cherish forever."

"Okay. But hurry. I'll feel better when you're here. You're always so calm, Lexie."

After a few more reassurances, she ended the call and let out a long breath.

"So, you call your own shots, huh?" Grayson asked with amusement in his voice. "It seems to me like you've traded one demanding client base for another, one with a lower retainer and more emotional drama."

As much as she hated to admit it, there was truth in his observation—and it struck uncomfortably close to home. "It's still different," she grumbled.

"How so?"

"I'm creating something meaningful. Something that brings people joy. The photos I take will remind them of the happiest day of their lives."

"But is it the happiest day of your life? And is it worth the pay cut? The stress? Having your weekends commandeered by strangers' emotional crises?"

"Yes," she said firmly, though a tiny voice in her head whispered otherwise. "Not that I expect someone like you to understand."

"Someone like me?" he echoed, shooting her a sharp glance.

"Someone who measures everything by its monetary value. Someone who sees a building full of people's homes and only thinks about profit margins. What he can gain, not what everyone else will lose."

His jaw tightened. "You don't know anything about me or what I value, Lexie."

"I know enough," she said, though a small part of her recognized the unfairness of her assessment. She barely knew Grayson Holt. But she did know he and his father ran a huge real-estate development company that was worth billions, which made her angry that they couldn't handle having one apartment building in their portfolio that might not be making them a lot of money but was still bringing in some profit.

Her phone rang again, sparing her from further debate. This time, it was the wedding planner, frantic about the timeline and double-checking when Lexie would arrive.

As she fielded another call immediately after—the best man wanting to know if she could get some epic shots of the groomsmen—Grayson remained silent, but she could feel his judgment radiating across the console.

"It's hectic now, but it's all going to work out," she said.

"Are you talking to me or to yourself?" he asked.

"I can feel you judging me."

"It's more that I'm curious why you made such a drastic

change in your life. I can't imagine your father was happy about that. Didn't he try to talk you out of leaving?"

"Yes, but I didn't want to be talked out of it. The truth is that I went into law because of him. I wanted to be close to him. I wanted us to have something in common. And he was so proud of me when I became a lawyer and joined his firm. But the reality of working as an associate in his firm was completely different than what I thought it would be. I was working eighty hours a week on deals that didn't seem at all important to me. I lasted almost two years before I quit. I gave it more than a fair shot, but it wasn't the career for me. I hoped he'd understand, but he didn't. I shouldn't have been surprised. His attention always came with strings. Now that I've let him down, he barely speaks to me."

"Huh. That's..." Grayson's voice trailed off.

"That's what?" she asked curiously.

"Interesting. We actually have something in common, fathers we wanted to connect with through work…and strings."

She met his gaze. "That's right. Your father is the reason you're staying at Ocean Shores for a month."

"He is. My dad seems to think I'll change my mind about wanting to sell the building when I get to know all the tenants."

"Your father might be right."

"I don't believe he is. And I'm betting you probably didn't think any of the strings your father placed on you were right, either."

"Maybe not," she admitted. "But this is different. Our community is special, and whether we can change your mind or not, I hope you'll at least get to know us, enjoy your time at Ocean Shores, because it could be the best month of your life."

He gave her a disbelieving smile. "I'm supposed to spend a month in Italy this summer. You think Ocean Shores can beat that?"

She nodded. "I think it can, but only if you have an open mind."

"You don't lack confidence, Lexie."

"Neither do you, Grayson," she said, deliberately using his first name since he'd used hers and also because she wanted him to start seeing her as an equal, not a tenant at one of his buildings. "I guess that's two things we have in common," she added as he turned into the entrance for the resort and pulled up in front of the main building. "Thanks for the ride."

"Good luck with the wedding," he said as she got out of the car.

She grabbed her equipment out of the trunk, hearing the wedding planner practically scream her name as she rushed out of the main entrance. Clearly, she'd been waiting for her. She closed the trunk and put on a professional smile.

She might not be doing exactly what she wanted, but she was taking steps in that direction. She couldn't let Grayson's doubts get into her head. She had too much to do.

But as she followed the wedding planner into the resort, she couldn't help wondering if she was calling her own shots. Or just pretending she was.

———

Grayson made his way through a grueling workout at a gym not far from Ocean Shores, which had turned out to be more impressive than its online photos. His workouts were his stress relievers. Pushing his body to a physical limit usually calmed his mind, but it hadn't worked today. His thoughts kept drifting back to the beautiful brunette he'd dropped off at the Seaside Cliff Resort.

Lexie Price was a pretty picture of contradictions, a woman he couldn't quite figure out. She'd annoyed him from the first minute they'd met, and that irritation had only grown when she'd sent him financial projections from one of the residents, along with another pitch to keep Ocean Shores off the market.

At the same time, he had admired her persistence. But he

hadn't really bothered to look at her friend's report or listen to her concerns, because he knew that he was going to sell the building as soon as he could. Now, he also knew that he was going to have to spend the next four weeks with her as a thorn in his side. It had been easy to dismiss her from afar, but in person, it was a lot more difficult.

She was beautiful for one thing, which had been impossible not to notice when she was wearing that skimpy hot pink bikini. But even in her work clothes, her dark-brown eyes and enticing features had made it hard to look away from her. Besides being way too attractive for his liking, she was also proud, fiery, and stubborn, and she was not going down without a fight. He didn't want a fight. He just wanted to sell and move on.

Unfortunately, that wasn't going to happen for a while.

On his way back to Ocean Shores from the gym, he tried to focus on the deals he was currently working on. He could dive into those as soon as he got back to his apartment. He had more than enough business to occupy his mind, but he felt strangely restless in this new city, this somewhat odd environment he'd found himself in.

For the past decade, he'd been running at a breakneck pace, living a life focused on furthering his business goals. Now he was hanging out at a beachside apartment where life definitely seemed to move at a slower pace. He didn't really care that his accommodations were modest. Lexie might believe he was a snob, but that wasn't really it. He just wanted to be the best at what he did, and moving real estate was part of that.

After parking his car in the lot, he got out and walked toward the entrance to the courtyard, pausing in surprise when he saw an older man with his head under the hood of a classic Mustang. That was a classic car he hadn't seen in a while.

The man pulled his head out and gave him a smile. "Hello," he said.

"Nice car."

"She will be even prettier when I'm done with her," the man

said, patting the fender of what appeared to be a 1967 Mustang convertible with faded red paint. "I'm Frank Wickham."

"Grayson Holt."

"Grayson Holt? I've heard of you. You're the new owner."

"Not exactly new. My father has owned this place for a long time, but I have recently taken over management of the property."

"So, you are the one in charge."

He wished he could say he was, but his father was still hanging on by his fingertips. Since he didn't want to get into that, he just said, "Yes. I assume you live here as well."

"I do. Josie threw me a lifeline after my wife died, and I decided to retire from my job as a corporate lawyer. I needed a place to start fresh. Moved in almost two years ago now. Changed my life."

"How's that?"

"It's hard to say exactly. But I have a simpler life now, and my friendships have more substance. I guess I found myself coming back to my roots. Last time I fixed up an old car was probably thirty years ago, when my son was seven or eight." Frank's gaze softened. "Bradley loved cars, still does, but he lives on the other side of the country now, so we don't share that hobby anymore. Truth be told, I got so busy with my job I stopped making the time to work on cars with him. I wish now I hadn't let that time go. When you get older, you realize that some choices have consequences you never imagined."

Frank's story brought back an old memory. When he'd been eight years old, he'd spent a lot of time in the garage of their Bel Air estate, watching his father's driver, Miguel, work on his father's collection of vintage cars. Miguel had been patient with him, letting him hand over tools, explaining how engines worked. Those summer afternoons had broken up some of the loneliness he'd felt growing up in a house with two very busy parents. Clearing his throat, he pushed that memory out of his head, focusing on the car in front of him.

"How long have you had this car?"

"A couple of months. I found her rusting in a barn in Temecula. The previous owner wanted to scrap her, but I saw the potential. I'm getting her ready for a car show in three weeks. It's going to be tight, but I've always liked a challenge." Frank ran his hand along the hood with obvious affection.

"Mind if I take a look?" The question surprised him as much as it seemed to surprise Frank.

"Not at all."

He stepped closer, noting the rust spots, the torn convertible top, the cracked dashboard visible through the windshield. It should have looked like a money pit. Instead, he found himself oddly drawn to the classic lines, the potential hidden beneath the neglect. "My father had a car like this, same color, a year older. I think you can bring her back to life."

"Your dad worked on cars?"

"He bought vintage cars. His driver worked on them, and I used to help him." He frowned, wondering why he was sharing this with a complete stranger.

"Well, I could use an extra set of hands if you have some time." Frank picked up a wrench from the small table he'd set up nearby. "I'm replacing the carburetor today, if you want to stick around, but it will be messy work."

He should say no. He had emails to return, calls to make, spreadsheets to review. His father might have forced him into this month-long exile, but that didn't mean he had to waste time playing mechanic with a retired lawyer and a broken-down Mustang.

But something about the invitation tugged at him. Maybe it was the memory of Miguel's patient explanations, or the way Frank's eyes had saddened when he'd mentioned working on cars with his son. Or maybe it was just the strange restlessness he'd been feeling since arriving at Ocean Shores, like he was waiting for something he couldn't name.

"I could help for a while," he said, almost immediately regretting the words, but it was too late to take his offer back.

"Great, but you should probably change your clothes."

"I'll be back in a few minutes." As he headed into the building, he caught sight of Lexie's car still sitting in the parking lot, lifeless, and made a mental note to ask Frank if he had some jumper cables.

The thought of Lexie brought back their earlier conversation, where she had accused him of only measuring things by their monetary value. She wasn't completely wrong, and that bothered him, because he didn't want to be that kind of person. He didn't want to only be about money, and maybe working on Frank's car was a way to prove that to himself. Spending time doing something physical would hopefully take his mind off not only work, but also one very irritating and intriguing brunette.

CHAPTER THREE

"Thanks again for rescuing me, Kaia," Lexie said as Kaia pulled into the Ocean Shores parking lot and turned off the engine late Saturday afternoon. "I owe you. Can I take you out to dinner tonight?"

"Actually, I have a date," Kaia said, giving her a sparkly smile.

"Really? Who's the lucky guy?"

"A doctor at the hospital where I drop off patients. He's asked me out a few times, and I finally decided to say yes."

"What took you so long?"

Kaia shrugged, a frown marring her features. "I don't know. I had such a bad date three weeks ago, and I just didn't feel like trying again."

"The guy who keeps texting you?" she asked with concern. "Is that still going on? Do we need to do something to get that to stop? Maybe you should talk to Ben."

"I think he's finally stopped. I haven't heard from him in a couple of days. And the last thing I want to do is talk to my brother about a bad date."

"But Ben's a cop. He could make sure this guy knows who he's messing with."

"I don't need Ben to fight my battles."

Lexie knew Kaia was fiercely proud, and growing up with her dad and two brothers had made her tough. But sometimes pride and toughness weren't enough. "Well, promise me that you'll tell me if you start feeling uncomfortable again, even if you don't want to tell Ben."

"It won't be a problem, Lexie. Don't worry about it. I shouldn't have even mentioned it. And I am moving on tonight with hopefully someone much more interesting."

"What's this doctor like?"

"If we have a good time, I'll tell you more about him tomorrow," she promised.

"You better. And hopefully, tonight will be just what the doctor ordered."

Kaia laughed. "Always the optimist, Lexie."

"It's better than always anticipating the worst."

"True. What about you? What are your plans?"

"I'm going to take off my heels and relax. It was a hellish day."

"For you or the bride?"

"For me. The bride ended up as happy as could be after multiple mishaps that I managed to handle without her knowing."

"Weren't you just there to take pictures?"

"I thought so, but my job seems to encompass a lot more than that. But it's over now. So, I don't want to think about it anymore."

As they got out of the car, she grabbed her equipment from the back seat, then heard Frank's distinctive laugh and another male voice. Moving around the car, she was shocked to see Grayson Holt bent over the engine of Frank's Mustang, his expensive workout clothes replaced by a faded T-shirt and jeans that had definitely seen better days. Oil streaked his forearms, and his usually perfect hair was disheveled. He was holding some kind of tool while Frank pointed at something in the engine compartment, both men completely absorbed in their work.

"Well, that's unexpected," Kaia murmured, following her gaze.

"I'll say. Grayson," she called out, impulsively, too surprised to stop herself.

He jerked upright at the sound of his name, his head connecting solidly with the raised hood of the car. The sharp crack echoed across the parking lot.

"Damn," he muttered, one hand immediately going to his forehead.

"Oh no!" She dropped her camera equipment and rushed over as remorse ran through her. "I'm so sorry! I didn't mean to startle you."

"You should put some ice on that," Frank said, eyeing the rapidly forming bump on Grayson's forehead with concern.

"I'll be fine," Grayson said, his lips drawing into a tight line that was probably a mix of anger and pain.

Kaia stepped up. "I'm a paramedic. Kaia Mercer—we met last night—sort of. Frank's right. You need ice. It's starting to swell."

"I'll do that," he said.

"Do you think he should get it checked?" she asked Kaia. "Maybe he has a concussion."

"I don't think it's that bad," Kaia said.

"It's not," Grayson said firmly. "It's just a bump."

"We should probably call it a day anyway," Frank said.

Grayson nodded, still pressing his palm against the injury. "All right."

"But if you want to help me tomorrow, I wouldn't say no," Frank added. "It was sure nice to have an extra set of hands, Grayson."

"I'll see. I'm not sure of my schedule." He handed a tool back to Frank. "I'll let you know."

After Grayson headed into the building, she turned to Frank. "How did you get Grayson involved in this?"

Frank shrugged. "He got himself involved. Came over and

started asking questions. He used to work on cars when he was a kid. Since he seemed interested in helping me, I let him. It was going well, too, until you arrived," he added with a twinkle in his eyes. "You distracted him, Lexie."

Heat crept up her neck. "I didn't mean to. I was just so surprised to see him out of his suit and tie. And it seems very odd that he used to work on cars. His family is wealthy."

"He said the vintage vehicles belonged to his father, but the man who taught him how to restore them was his dad's driver."

"Well, that makes more sense. Did he say anything about selling the building?"

"We didn't get into that. We talked about the engine mostly. He's a smart guy, good with his hands, too. And very focused. But his mind went elsewhere when he heard your voice."

"And now he has a bump on his head," she said with a sigh. "That I caused. His stay here is definitely not going as well as I'd hoped."

"He'll be okay," Kaia reassured her. "And it's not like you did anything, Lexie. You just said his name, and he jumped. It was more his fault than yours."

"I wouldn't worry about it," Frank added as he put away his tools. "I don't think that bump is going to factor into his decision."

"Maybe helping you will. I'm glad you got him doing something he obviously enjoyed."

"It was nice to have the help. He reminded me a little of my son."

She hadn't anticipated that Frank would be the first one to find a connection with Grayson, but she was very glad it had happened.

"I should go inside," Kaia said. "I need to take a shower."

"I'm coming, too." She retrieved her camera equipment and walked into the courtyard with Kaia. "I can't believe Grayson was working with Frank on his car. He had oil on his jeans and on his hands, and before today, I would have thought he was a man who wouldn't allow a piece of lint to cling to his suit jacket."

"I thought this version of him was hot," Kaia said with a smile. "You like him, don't you, Lexie?"

"God, no! The man is trying to take away our home. I don't like him at all."

"You don't want to like him, but—"

"No buts. I'm just trying to figure him out. I need to know who he is so I can find a way to change his mind. Since my plan of charming the hell out of him is not working very well, I might need to think of another approach. Anyway, thanks again for the ride, and have fun on your date. Tomorrow, I want details."

"If there's anything worth sharing, you'll be my first call."

After parting ways with Kaia, she headed into her first-floor apartment. Dropping her bags on the coffee table, she kicked off her shoes and flopped onto the couch for several long minutes, debating her next move. She'd planned to put on her sweats, heat up some leftovers, and find a movie to watch, but she couldn't stop thinking about Grayson and the injury she'd caused.

Getting up, she moved into the kitchen and opened the freezer. The ice pack she'd used when she'd pulled a muscle last week was right on the shelf. The least she could do was take him some ice and apologize again. Ignoring the fact that he probably had plenty of ice in his own freezer, she grabbed the pack and headed outside and up the stairs.

Grayson answered her knock, still wearing his same dirty clothes, faint streaks of oil still on his hands and forearms. The bump on his forehead was definitely swelling and turning purple.

"Ice pack," she said, holding it up. "For your head. I feel terrible about startling you."

"That's not necessary. I was just going to throw some ice in a towel."

"Well, this is better." She studied his head with concern. "I could take you to urgent care, if you want to get it checked out."

"Lexie, I'm fine. Stop worrying. In fact, why are you worrying?" he asked, sending her a speculative look. "You hate my guts, don't you? Seems like you'd be more concerned about the damage to the hood of that car than to my head."

"I wouldn't say I hate you. That's a little strong. And I certainly don't want to see you hurt."

"Afraid I'll hold it against you? That it will make me want to sell even more?"

She let out a breath, thinking this move was a mistake. "Believe it or not, I just wanted to make sure you were all right. I didn't think about it beyond that. You were nice enough to give me a ride to the wedding this morning, and I felt guilty for surprising you and making you bump your head. That's it." She held out the ice pack. "Take it or leave it."

He took it from her hand. "Thank you."

She could leave, but instead, she lingered in his doorway. "I was surprised to see you working on Frank's car. You don't seem like a man who likes to get his hands dirty."

"Like I told you this morning, you don't know anything about me."

"I guess I believe that more now. Just like you don't know that much about me. We've both made assumptions, wouldn't you say?"

"Probably." His gaze dropped to her shirt, tipping his head at the purple stain streaking across her blouse. "Rough day at the wedding?"

She glanced down and then nodded. "Three-year-old with purple icing on her very sticky fingers."

"Sounds like fun."

"Fun isn't the word I'd use. But it's over, and I got great shots. In the end, everyone will be happy with the pictures."

"Then it was a successful job."

"It was."

"Good. By the way, I told Frank your battery was dead. He

gave me jumper cables, and I put them in the back of my car. I can give you a jump, if you want."

Heat flooded her cheeks as his innocent offer sent her mind in a direction that it shouldn't go. Clearing her throat, she said, "That would be great. But you should rest your head. You don't need to do that now."

"Why don't you give me an hour to clean up, and then we can get your car running?" he suggested.

She was surprised again by his generous offer. "Are you sure you're up to it?"

"I am, and I suspect you're going to need your car at some point."

"Tomorrow morning, in fact," she admitted.

"Then let's do it tonight. Unless you have other plans. You will need to drive it around for a while to charge the battery. Are you up for that?"

"Sure." She hesitated again, then said, "Since I'll have to drive somewhere, do you want to come with me? I can take you to dinner. There's this great new restaurant that two of our residents, Madison and Gabe, opened last year. They usually work Saturday nights. You could meet them, and their food is fantastic." Grayson didn't immediately respond, and she couldn't help pushing. "I owe you for the ride this morning and for helping me with the car. Please say yes. I don't really want to owe you."

A slow smile spread across his face at her words. "In that case, I will say yes. Then we'll be even."

"I'll meet you in the parking lot in an hour."

"See you then."

As she turned away from his door, she felt both happy and worried about her impulsive invitation. But considering how bad things had gone so far, tonight could only be better. At least, that was the hope...

CHAPTER FOUR

An hour later, Grayson grabbed Frank's jumper cables from the trunk of his car as he questioned his decision to accept Lexie's dinner invitation. He'd showered, changed into dark jeans and a button-down shirt, and tried to convince himself this was simply a good business strategy. Getting to know Lexie and the other residents would help him craft a more compelling relocation package when the time came.

At least, that's what he told himself. But as Lexie emerged from the building in a sundress that somehow managed to be both casual and elegant, dark-brown hair flowing in beautiful waves over her shoulder, her face lit up by the setting sun, he knew his interest in her went beyond business. He found himself staring at her far longer than was appropriate.

"Ready?" she asked, pulling her keys from her purse.

Her words kicked his brain back into gear. "Yes. Let's see if we can bring your car back to life."

She popped the hood of her Honda and slid behind the wheel while he connected the cables. "Try it now," he said.

The engine turned over on the second try.

"Thank you," she said, genuine gratitude in her voice as he

removed the cables. "I was a little afraid it still wasn't going to start."

"Well, I wouldn't celebrate too fast. You might still need a new battery."

"I'm hoping to push that expense off for a while."

He put the cables in the back of her car, then got into the passenger seat. She gave him an apologetic smile. "Sorry we have to take my car. It's not as nice as yours."

"It's fine." As he settled into his seat, he glanced around the vehicle, noting the camera lens in the cup holder and two photography magazines on the passenger-side floorboard, which she quickly grabbed and tossed in the back.

"So," she said as they pulled out of the parking lot, "Frank said you were a big help today. I had no idea you were an auto mechanic."

"That's a stretch. I'm more of a hobbyist. My father collected vintage automobiles. His driver, Miguel, maintained them, and I used to help him. Actually, I probably got in the way more than I helped, but he was a kind man, and he was patient with me. Although he did work for my father, so he probably thought that was part of the job," he added dryly.

"How many cars did your dad have?"

"Three or four at any given time. My dad rarely let me ride in them. They were more for show than anything else."

"Have you followed in his footsteps? Do you have your own fleet of restored cars?"

"No. I lost interest in that a long time ago," he murmured.

"Why? It sounds like it was something you enjoyed."

"Do you always ask so many questions?"

"That's not an answer. And you said I don't know you at all, so I'm trying to find out more," she said pointedly.

He smiled. "Okay. As I got older, my parents moved around more. We lived in different cities, sometimes different countries, and we didn't spend much time at the house in Bel Air, where most of the cars were." He shrugged. "I got into other things."

"Did you live in Europe?"

"Yes. We had a house in London, one in Paris, and a villa in Tuscany."

"Wow. That's amazing. What a life you've led."

Through her big, beautiful eyes, he actually found a new appreciation for that life. "I definitely had a lot of good experiences traveling. But I hated the sudden endings to some of our travels. I'd just be starting to make friends, and we'd be on to somewhere else." He stopped abruptly, feeling like he was revealing too much.

"I would love to go to Italy, and not just the touristy areas. I'd like to get off the beaten track and take pictures of those small villages, the seaside cafes, the lemon trees. There's something about the majesty of the architecture, mirrored by the majesty of the Italian Alps, that really appeals to me."

"It is a beautiful country," he agreed. "Have you done much traveling, Lexie?"

"My parents took me to London and Paris when I was a teenager, but that was for two weeks, and we didn't even get out of those cities to see anything else. My father was there on business, and we tagged along."

"Your mother didn't want to sightsee?"

"Only in beautiful stores like Harrods. She loves to shop. That's her idea of a good time. Not so much mine."

"Do you have siblings?"

"No, it's just me. My parents weren't really into kids; it was just part of the whole marriage and family experience they felt they should have so they would be like everyone else. But they were busy with their own lives, and I spent most of my time with a parade of nannies."

"I know what that's like," he muttered, reminded that while she might drive an old car now and live in an apartment, she hadn't grown up poor.

"I never had a driver, though," she said, flashing him a smile. "My father is very successful but not at the level of your dad."

She paused. "What about you? Are you and your parents close? You don't have any siblings, either, do you?"

"No. Like your parents, they had an obligatory child, but that's where the interest ended."

She gave him a quick look. "Something else we have in common."

"True. But I still work with my father, while you do not."

"Your father is probably easier to work for. He clearly respects you and wants you to take over his company. My father treated me like every other associate at his firm, and if I did something wrong, he would blow up, as if my mistake was a reflection of him. I don't think he had much respect for my abilities."

"He might have just wanted you to prove yourself."

"That's what he said. He wasn't going to give me any favors, and that was fine. But I also think he treated me more harshly just to prove the point, which wasn't necessary. I hoped that quitting might actually improve our relationship, but he just can't get over the anger and disappointment he feels toward me. Maybe one day that will change, but I'm not holding my breath. How is it working with your dad?"

"I paid my dues in the company, starting at the bottom. I worked every entry-level job from the time I was eighteen on. He wanted me to know how to do everything, or at least know how it was being done by others. It was a smart move, even though I was often impatient with my slow progress. But having that foundation helped me when I graduated from college and got my MBA. I was really ready then to move into a leadership position." He paused. "My father and I were not close when I was growing up. And we did get closer when I went to work for him, but even that took years. It really wasn't until about two years ago, when he finally decided to slow down, that we started to talk more about how I could take over his business. Since then, we've been getting along well, except when he makes strange requests that he doesn't care to explain."

"Like having to spend a month at Ocean Shores?" she asked with a smile.

"Exactly."

"Why did he want you to spend time with us?"

"He has not explained his reasoning to me. I've never seen him care about any company that he owns, so why he has any sentiment about your apartment building is a mystery to me."

"My aunt seems rather mysterious about your presence in the building, too, almost like she has some idea of why your father asked you to come but doesn't want to say. I wonder if he told her, but not you."

"I honestly have no idea."

"Well, hopefully, it won't be a horrible month. You do get to live right next to the ocean. There are some perks."

"That's true." He paused as she pulled into the restaurant parking lot. "This looks interesting."

"I love the building, but the food is even better." Sol y Mar occupied a converted beach house, its weathered cedar shingles and expansive deck giving it the casual elegance of a well-loved summer cottage. String lights wrapped around the railings, and the sound of waves was clearly audible even from the parking lot. "Madison and Gabe opened this place about nine months ago, and it's always packed. They got a lot of attention when they appeared on a TV cooking competition last year, where they were pitted against each other."

"That sounds interesting."

"It was definitely that. Madison is classically trained in French cuisine and was running an upscale restaurant, while Gabe is a self-taught chef whose Mexican roots often appear in his cooking, and he was working a food truck that was parked down the street from her restaurant. They actually disliked each other intensely when they first met. But while they were opposites in every way, when they started cooking together, they found a synergy and a magic that not only created a great professional partnership but a personal one as well. They're getting married this summer."

"Sounds like they found a happy ending."

"Yes, but it's not an ending according to Gabe, it's just the beginning." She paused. "Do you think it's okay to turn the engine off? I'm almost afraid to do it in case it dies again."

"I think we're good. If not, we'll jump it again. The cables are in the back."

"You're right. I'm not going to worry about it."

She turned off the engine, and they got out of the car and walked into the restaurant. The interior was as charmingly warm and inviting as the outside, with exposed beams, local artwork on cream-colored walls, and tables that looked like they'd been crafted by local artisans rather than ordered from a restaurant supply catalog.

"Hello, Lexie," the hostess said before giving him a curious look. "I've got the perfect table for you and your friend."

"Thanks," Lexie said. "But I don't think there's a bad table in this place."

The hostess motioned to a young man who took them through the restaurant and out another door onto a covered deck that was cozy and warm but also offered a spectacular view of the ocean. They'd barely sat down when a dark-haired, dark-eyed man wearing a chef's coat came over to the table.

"Hi, Lex," he said, then turned his gaze to him. "Mr. Holt. I'm Gabe Herrera. My fiancée, Madison, and I live right next door to you in 12B."

"Nice to meet you."

"I'm glad Lexie brought you in. If you don't mind, I'd love to treat you both to some special dishes we're making tonight. Of course, you can also pick from the menu, if you'd prefer that."

He wasn't usually that into surprises. He preferred to order what he wanted. He liked predictability, but judging by the expressions on both their faces, that was clearly not the correct answer. "Sure," he said. "I'd love to eat whatever you choose to serve."

"Great. Any allergies or dislikes?"

"Nope."

"That makes it easy," Gabe said, picking up their menus. "Madison will be out in a while to say hello. And the waiter will take your drink orders shortly."

"I love the view from here," Lexie said as Gabe left them alone. "It's too bad the sun has already set, but we still have a painted sky."

The sky was a mix of fading orange, pink, and purple, casting a glow over the water. "I'm surprised you're not taking a photograph," he said, looking back at her.

"I've taken a million shots of the sunrises and sunsets around here. I don't need more."

"Do you sell your photographs or show them somewhere?"

"I've been talking to a gallery in town about a show, but I don't have quite the collection I want yet."

"What are you waiting for?"

She frowned, bristling a little at his question. "I'm not waiting for anything. I've just been busy. I have a lot of jobs right now, and I help my aunt at Ocean Shores, and it's just...busy." She picked up her water glass and took a sip.

"Okay."

Judging by the spark of fire in her eyes, she didn't like that comment any more than she'd liked his question.

"I will have a show," she said firmly. "But I'm not going to do it half-assed. I want it to be perfect, the best it can be."

"Are you trying to convince me or yourself?" he challenged.

"I don't have to convince you of anything."

"You don't. But it feels like there's something stopping you besides time."

A frown turned down her mouth. Then she said, "I want to show photographs that are different, that make people think, that create emotion and feeling. It's important to me to put out something great, not just good enough. And I don't have enough photographs that fit that description."

The passion in her voice told him far more than her words. She had bigger ambitions than he'd realized, and she also didn't like to fail. "Then you're smart to wait until you have exactly what you want."

"I think so. And I appreciate you saying that, even though you probably don't think much of my business acumen in turning down a great opportunity like this."

"I don't know enough about your acumen to make an assessment," he said with a light smile.

She reluctantly smiled back. "And we're not going to get into that tonight." She paused as the waiter delivered a very expensive bottle of wine to their table. "Gabe is pulling out all the stops."

"The chefs insist that this will complement the meal," the waiter said. "Do you want to taste it first?"

"No, please just pour," she said. "I trust Madison and Gabe."

The waiter filled their glasses and told them their appetizer would be out shortly.

"This is good," he said, taking a sip of the merlot. "Your friends are very generous. They must like you a lot."

"I think this is about impressing you."

"To save the building," he said with a nod. "I'm very aware of the ground game, Lexie, and I know you won't believe me when I tell you that this isn't personal, but it really isn't. I'm not trying to hurt anyone."

"But that would be the result," she argued.

"Life is about change. Sometimes moving on is a good thing. A different location can give you a different perspective." He frowned as he finished speaking.

"See, even you couldn't get through that with a straight face," she said, giving him a pointed look.

"Actually, I was just thinking that I was repeating someone else's words."

"Whose?" she asked curiously.

"My mother. Funny, it's usually my dad's voice that rings through my head, but that was all her. Every time we moved, and I complained, she pointed out all the positives."

"Did you believe her?"

He met her gaze. "No. But she wasn't always wrong."

"Always?" she echoed. "But sometimes?"

"Sometimes," he admitted. He shook his head in bemusement. "I never really thought her words would come out of my mouth." He took a long sip of wine.

"That has happened a few times to me, too," she said with a laugh. "It shocks me every time, and I don't like it at all."

"I'll drink to that," he said, raising his glass.

She picked up her glass and clinked it against his. "Cheers." As she set her glass down, the waiter appeared with their appetizer.

"You have three perfectly seared scallops perched on a bed of silky corn purée and roasted poblano chili with a citrus beurre blanc and a blue corn tuile. Enjoy," the waiter said.

As the man left, he said, "I didn't get all that, but it sounds impressive."

"It tastes even better. Gabe created it a few weeks ago. I've already had it once, and it's unforgettable."

He felt a little guilty that her friends were going all out for him when he wasn't going to base his decision on one incredible meal. "Maybe you should tell your friends that they don't need to try—" he began.

Lexie cut him off with a shake of her head. "Just enjoy. There aren't any strings."

"In my experience, everything comes with strings."

"That used to be my experience, too, when I was surrounded by lawyers and other sharks, but not anymore. The people at Ocean Shores are good people, and all Madison and Gabe want is for you to enjoy their food. So, let's do that, because I'm starving, and it's been a long day."

He relaxed at her words. "That sounds good to me."

A relaxed Grayson Holt was even more attractive, Lexie couldn't help thinking as she half listened to a story he was telling about his encounter with a stubborn sheep on a lonely road in Ireland.

"How did you finally get it to move?" she asked.

A gleam entered his eyes. "I whispered something in her ear."

"Really?" She definitely liked this more lighthearted side of him. "What did you whisper?"

"It's between me and her."

"Sweet, lying promises," she suggested.

"Sweet but not lying. I told her that I'd walk with her and find her a better spot to graze, so I walked down the road, and she followed. Eventually, I moved her onto the grass, and my driver picked me up."

The image of him walking a sheep down the road made her smile. "I have to admit, I'm surprised by your level of patience. I wouldn't have thought you had that in you."

"She was a test of my patience because she kept stopping, and I had to keep telling her we needed to go."

"In the end, you got what you wanted."

"I usually do," he admitted.

That reminder drove the smile from her face, but she didn't say that he wasn't going to get his way this time because that would make him try harder to prove her wrong. Instead, she'd take a page from his book and walk him a little farther down the road. That thought put the smile back on her lips.

Grayson gave her an inquisitive look. "What are you thinking?"

"That I wish I could have photographed you and that sheep on that lonely road in Ireland. Did anyone take a photo?"

"No. I'm not someone who immortalizes my every moment with a picture."

"Too bad. Because that would have been a moment worth capturing." She picked up her wineglass and took a sip.

"I hope you didn't take that as an insult," he said quickly. "I wasn't talking about you as a professional photographer; I was thinking about one of the women I used to see who only ordered food she could photograph, and half the time she didn't even like it. It made no sense to me."

"I'm not interested in food photography, either. Although that appetizer we just ate was definitely worth a post on social media, and I did take a photo of it the first time I ate it because I want people to see how good the food is here."

"I would have made an exception for that, too," he conceded. "It was ridiculously good, and I can't wait to see what we're getting next."

"It will be spectacular. Neither Madison nor Gabe believes in mediocrity, not when it comes to food. And even though they're on the same team now, they push each other to be better."

"I like their commitment to excellence. Too many people settle for average or good enough."

As Grayson finished talking, two waiters delivered their meals, with Madison arriving at the table, her face flushed, and her blonde hair pulled back from her face.

"Lexie, I'm so glad you brought Mr. Holt here. I'm Madison Baldwin."

"Nice to meet you," he said. "And I'm very impressed with the food."

"The appetizer was all Gabe. This course is mine," she said with a proud smile. "I hope you like fish. I've prepared a pan-roasted halibut on a saffron-infused risotto with fresh sweet crab and grilled asparagus, with a dusting of smoky ancho chili salt. The fish was caught this morning, so it's about as fresh as it can be."

"I can't wait," he said.

"Please, eat," she said with a wave of her hand. "And let your waiter know if you need anything else."

As Madison left, they both dug in and spent the next several minutes eating in comfortable silence. She hadn't had this particular dish before, and she loved the creaminess of the risotto with the salty pop of crab and melt-in-your-mouth fresh halibut. She wanted to ask Grayson what he thought, but there was no need because he was eating with genuine enthusiasm.

Everything was absolutely perfect: the incredible food, the amazing view, and the interesting man sitting across from her. The hectic mania of the wedding had completely disappeared from her mind, and she couldn't help wishing that more of her days ended like this.

Grayson didn't say a word until he had cleaned his plate. Then he leaned back and gave her a sheepish smile. "Sorry."

"For what?" she asked curiously.

"Not talking for the last twenty minutes."

"That was just a testament to the food, and, clearly, I was right there with you." She finished her last bite and wiped her mouth with a napkin. "That was excellent."

"Your friends are very talented. I can see why this place is packed."

"It's getting more popular every day, but I think they still have some nights that are slower than they would like. According to them, that's the restaurant business."

"One of the toughest businesses," he said. "My father invested in several restaurants, but only one of the three is still open. The other two didn't last more than a year. So, we don't invest in restaurants anymore."

"What if you tasted something amazing and the restaurant needed financial help? You wouldn't be tempted to invest?"

"Great food is one thing. What matters most is the bottom line."

She frowned at that reminder. "Do you ever stop thinking about the bottom line? You can't measure the value of everything by dollars and cents."

"You can, from an investment standpoint. And I thought we weren't talking about business tonight."

"You're right." She reminded herself she was supposed to be walking her sheep down the road, not yelling at it to do the right thing.

Before either of them could speak again, the waiter cleared their plates, and Gabe returned with dessert, setting it down between them. A molten chocolate cake, its shell just firm enough to hold in the lava of ganache, was paired with a scoop of coconut gelato topped with candied pepitas.

She broke into it with her spoon, the chocolate flowing out like a secret, and she took a sweet bite, thinking this might be the best thing yet.

"Oh, my God," she murmured.

"Oh, my God!" he echoed, meeting her gaze with a look of bemusement in his dark-brown eyes. "I didn't think they could top themselves, but they did."

"I agree. And I know this restaurant will be a long-term success."

"I don't doubt it," he said.

"I just hope Madison and Gabe won't be homeless at some point while they're sinking all their money into this place," she couldn't help adding.

Grayson shook his head. "And you just asked me if I ever stop..."

"Just giving you something to think about."

"Sorry, I can't think about anything except how good this is."

It wasn't what she wanted to hear, but it was enough for now.

CHAPTER FIVE

Grayson woke up early Sunday morning and went for a long run in the cool morning sunshine. The beach path was one of the most picturesque runs he'd done in a while. For the past few months, he'd only worked out in a gym, so it felt good to be outside, to be running to the beat of the crashing waves. It almost made him feel like he was on vacation, but he needed to stop that feeling in its tracks.

He was here to assess the Ocean Shores property and spend the designated amount of time on-site before he sold it. While he was here, he would not be relaxing, working on cars or having dinner with a pretty woman; he'd be staying on top of his business deals. He didn't want to miss a detail because he was distracted, and he'd been very distracted since he'd arrived. He would change that today.

When he returned, the courtyard was still empty, and he didn't pass anyone on his way up the stairs, which was a relief. He didn't have to meet someone new or engage in small talk. After taking a quick shower, he put on jeans and a T-shirt. Then he headed into the kitchen and made coffee, happy he'd packed his special coffee blend in his suitcase.

While the coffee was brewing, he made eggs and grabbed a

banana for breakfast, then sat down at his computer. He had three emails from Carrie, his admin, who was also working on a Sunday, despite his instructions to take the weekend off. But Carrie was as driven as he was. She'd forwarded several reports he'd requested, along with his revised calendar for the month.

A month. Thirty days of his life, sequestered in this apartment building because of his father's inexplicable whim.

He sighed at the thought, waiting for the familiar feeling of anger and frustration to wash over him, but instead his mind drifted to Lexie, to the enjoyable dinner they'd shared last night, to the conversation that had been both prickly at times and entertaining at others. That had been a surprise.

He hadn't expected to spend much time with Lexie. Their first interaction months ago had been an angry clash, and he knew she was going to fight him with everything she had to stop the sale of the building. So, he'd planned to stay away from her, but instead, he'd spent hours with her yesterday and had quickly discovered she was much more than just his most vocal opponent at Ocean Shores.

She was beautiful and intriguing, sharp-witted, and oddly easy to talk to. He'd always been able to categorize people, but Lexie defied classification. She was smart and a Georgetown-educated lawyer who'd walked away from a prestigious career to take photographs. Despite that free-spirited move, she hadn't completely left the world of financial obligations, taking on photography jobs to pay the bills, and presumably helping Josie for the same reason.

While she had elements of being a passionate rule breaker, Lexie also had a practical side, which added up to a very tantalizing puzzle, but definitely not one he should try to solve. That would take longer than four weeks, and that was the length of time he would be here.

There was no point in starting a friendship—or anything else—with her. He would be leaving in a month, and, at the end of the day, he would sell Ocean Shores, and she would probably end up hating him with every ounce of energy she had.

Thinking about the bottom line reminded him of her comments at dinner. He did look at his life, at his work, in terms of how everything added up, but there was nothing wrong with that. Living like Lexie, deluding herself with grand artistic visions while she did little to actually try to make those visions happen, was not a better way to live. Sure, she might have a bit more excitement, more freedom, more surprises, but he had stability, he had achievement, and closing deals was exciting, too. He was on the right track, and he wasn't going to let her assessment of his thinking change his mind.

He sighed again, knowing he needed to get her out of his head. It was time to work. He spent the next hour going over environmental reports for a building they planned to acquire in Chicago and then moved on to the proposal for a development deal in Singapore, something he'd been working on for several weeks, but negotiations had paused when the CEO of the company they were planning to work with fell ill, which stalled everything. He was concerned that the company might back out of the deal entirely, which meant he needed to come up with a backup plan.

Despite his best intentions to focus on work and nothing else, he got distracted every time he heard someone walk down the hall. It wasn't as loud as he'd thought it would be, but there was no way to really get away from the soft sounds of conversation or the quiet notes of laughter.

Obviously, the tenants liked that sense of inclusion. That feeling of not being alone. It was never too quiet. He supposed that could be a good thing. But not if you wanted to study or work or just think about your own life and not anyone else's. He'd grown up in big, almost silent houses, with multiple floors and far too many bedrooms for their small three-person family. He was more used to the echo of empty rooms than to the sound of people talking or laughing.

Knowing he wasn't getting much done, he got up from his computer and walked to the window. There was a palm tree that blocked most of his view of the courtyard, and while that was probably a good thing, it was also a little annoying that he couldn't see who was around. Not that it mattered who was around. He wasn't here to make friends, and it would make his life easier if he didn't get to know anyone too well, because then this whole deal would become personal.

Which made him wonder again why his father wanted him to see the building's tenants as people, as a community. His father had bought and sold plenty of buildings without giving the tenants a second thought, so why did he care so much about these people, about this place?

Maybe it was time to try to find an answer to that question. He hadn't had a chance to talk to the manager since he'd arrived. While Lexie had a lot to say on all subjects involving the building, her aunt was the official manager, and, ultimately, she was the one he'd be working with when it came time to sell.

Grabbing his keys, he left the apartment. As he came down the stairs, he saw an older woman sitting at a table working on the Sunday crossword. She gave him a smile.

"Good morning, Mr. Holt. I'm Margaret. Frank told me how you helped him with his car yesterday."

"I did. It's nice to meet you, Margaret."

"You, too. And fair warning, I think Frank is hoping to enlist your help today, too. I don't know if he told you, but he's planning to take that Mustang to a car show in a couple of weeks, and it's a long way from being ready."

"He mentioned that, and I'm happy to help, but maybe a little later. I need to talk to Josie."

"She should be home," Margaret said. "We're going to play bridge in an hour. Do you play?"

"No. Never have."

"Well, it's very easy to learn, and we're always looking for players."

"Uh, I'm not much of a card player."

"I'm sure a smart man like you would pick it up quickly. We also play poker. Of course, Josie and I aren't very good at it, but it's fun, and we even play for money," she said with a twinkle in her eyes.

"Don't let her hustle you," Kaia said as she moved toward them, wearing her paramedic's uniform. "Josie and Margaret took my brother, Ben, for almost fifty dollars the first week he moved in. They're sharks."

"Oh, now, that's not true," Margaret said with a laugh. "And I think Ben was just being a good sport. Letting two old ladies win a little money."

Kaia rolled her eyes as she smiled at him. "You've been warned, Mr. Holt."

"Thanks," he said. "Although I'm surprised you'd give me a warning."

"Well, Lexie wants you to enjoy your time here, which does not include getting sucked into a card game where you might lose money. Not that fifty bucks would put a dent in your wallet."

"We don't always win," Margaret interjected. "And we never cheat, Mr. Holt."

"I believe you. Maybe we'll play some cards before I go." He paused, turning back to Kaia. "Are you working today?"

"Yes, unfortunately. I'm filling in for someone who got sick last night." She checked her watch. "I better run. Have a nice day."

As Kaia left, he walked around the pool and knocked on Josie's door.

"Mr. Holt," Josie said, her eyebrows rising in surprise when she saw him. "I wasn't expecting you."

"Do you have a few minutes to talk?"

"Of course. Come in." She stepped back, gesturing him inside.

Josie's apartment was larger than the unit he'd been assigned, configured differently to accommodate a small office area. But what caught his attention was the décor—vibrant colors everywhere, eclectic furniture pieces that somehow worked together, and walls covered with framed photographs and movie posters. As his gaze swept the room, it caught on something gold and shiny, and when he moved closer to the shelf, he realized it was a very prestigious award.

"Is that an Oscar?" he asked.

"Yes, it is. I won Best Supporting Actress for the movie, *Heart of the Wolf*. I played a young single mother whose son befriends a wolf. It was thirty-eight years ago now. I'm sure you've never heard of the movie, and I doubt you've ever heard of me."

Grayson blinked in bemusement. "I had no idea you were an actress, or that you'd been in a movie and won an Oscar."

"I quit acting shortly after I got that award. I left Hollywood and moved here, and I've been here ever since. Can I get you something to drink?"

"No, I'm fine, thanks."

"Then, let's sit down." She waved him toward the couch, which was near a set of patio doors that opened into a small, enclosed deck filled with plants and also a hint of weed.

"Uh, is that smell what I think it is?"

Josie followed his gaze and laughed. "It's legal to grow plants for personal use, and it helps with my arthritis."

"Fair enough."

"What do you want to ask me?" she asked as they sat down on her comfortable couch.

"I just wanted to let you know that despite my residency here for the next month, I'm still planning to sell the building. However, we will have relocation packages for the tenants."

"You think money can replace the community they've built here?"

"Not replace but hopefully make their lives easier and provide an option for other opportunities."

"You sound exactly like your father." Josie tilted her head, studying him with uncomfortably perceptive eyes. "You're the spitting image of Emerson. Same eyes. Same way of walking into a room and taking charge of a conversation as if you own every room you enter. And you probably own a lot of them, don't you?"

"Some," he admitted. "How often have you talked to my father? I was under the impression that you worked with a manager in our company, Steve Robbins."

"Yes, I've worked with Steve since I first became manager, but I have had a few conversations with your father."

"He didn't mention that." He gave her a thoughtful look. "In one of those conversations, did my father mention why he wanted me to stay here for a month? It might be helpful if I could understand his reasoning."

"You should ask Emerson that question."

"He didn't want to answer."

"Well, that's between you and him."

"Okay," he said, realizing he wasn't going to get any information from her. "Can I ask you another question?"

"That depends on what it is."

"How do you feel about having to move?"

"With my fancy relocation package?" she asked with a wry but somewhat sad smile. "I'll survive if there's no other option."

"This is business; it's not personal," he said, wondering how many times he would have to tell people that.

"There are real people who live here."

"Which is why I don't usually get to know the people I'm going to force out of a building," he said bluntly. "And why I'm so confused my father felt it necessary for me to do that now. But I've known for the last several years that there is something about this building that holds value to him." He paused. "Would you disagree?"

"Like I said before, you'd have to ask him." She gave him a compassionate smile. "I'm sorry I can't be more forthcoming.

You're a man who likes answers, who wants things to add up, and this doesn't add up."

"It doesn't."

"I could do a Tarot card reading for you, if you want. It might clarify things."

"I don't believe in that."

"Well, that's not surprising. But if you change your mind, let me know. Is there anything else I can help you with? If you want to go over the financial records again, Lexie and I have organized everything for you, even better than it was the last time you visited. We've also rented two more apartments since then, so we have only one vacancy at the moment."

He knew all that. And it just didn't matter. The worth of the building came from its location, from how it could be developed. It was prime real estate, and he believed they could get top dollar for it. But all he said was, "Thanks. I think Lexie and Steve already sent me the latest figures, so I have what I need."

She got to her feet as he rose. "Sometimes what you think you need isn't what you really need, Grayson. You never know when life will take an unexpected turn, and the detour becomes the main road. That's what happened to me. I had no idea where I was going to end up when I left Hollywood. But I ended up here, and I have loved every minute of it. I found the family I never had."

"But Lexie is your actual family, right? So, you do have a family."

"Lexie's mother is my half-sister," Josie admitted. "I was nine when my sister came along, and we were never close. We are as different as two people can be, and my sister, Lexie's mother, absolutely hates that Lexie chose to live and work with me. But Lexie wasn't getting what she needed in her old life, and I think she's pretty happy now."

"It kind of sounds like you both ran away from something and ended up here. I don't like to leave my life to chance. I don't like to run away; I like to run toward something and get what I know I want, not what the universe decides to show me."

She smiled. "You are your father's son. And I suspect you'll make the same decision he did."

"He bought this building and still doesn't want to sell it. How is that the same decision?" At her pointed look, he added, "I need to ask him, right?"

"Or the Tarot cards."

"I'll start with him. Thanks."

"You're welcome. And whatever happens, Grayson, I hope you'll enjoy your time here. There's a lot of magic here. A lot of healing."

"I don't need magic or healing."

"Then you're luckier than most."

CHAPTER SIX

Grayson left Josie's apartment with a sour feeling in his gut. He knew he was lucky. He also knew he was privileged, and sometimes he'd wondered if he'd made the wrong decision working with his father, because it had put the nepotism label on his head. But he couldn't worry about that. His father had wanted him in the business, and he'd wanted the connection with his dad. He'd also worked damn hard to be good at his job. And he certainly didn't need a Tarot card reading to tell him what to do next. He was curious why his father had sent him to Ocean Shores, but he didn't need to know that answer to sell the building, which was what he would do at the end of his time here.

As he walked up the stairs to his apartment, he ran into a woman at the top, who was very pregnant and also balancing a basket of laundry.

"Let me help you with that," he said.

"If you wouldn't mind," she replied with relief as he took the basket out of her hands. "I underestimated how difficult it would be to manage the stairs with a laundry basket when I can barely see my feet."

"No problem. I take it you're headed to the laundry room."

"Yes. I'm Serena Morrison. I live just a few doors down from you with my husband, Brad. I don't know if you've met him yet. He runs Maverick's Bar and Grill."

"I haven't had the pleasure of meeting him or going to Maverick's, but I will check it out."

"You should. It's very popular," she said as she followed him slowly down the stairs and into the laundry room.

He set the basket on a table. "Here you go."

"Thanks. You're a lifesaver. Brad told me he'd do the laundry, but he had to run to the bar for some pipe emergency, and I really needed some clean clothes."

"Can I help you load the washer?"

"I can manage that. Have you had a chance to talk to my sister, Ava, yet?"

"No," he said. "But I think I read a report she wrote."

"Lexie had her do an analysis for you. She's great with numbers, and she's been working with venture capitalists and investment bankers for years, so she knows her stuff."

He didn't want to admit that he'd barely looked at the report. "I need to take another look at it," he said diplomatically.

"You should. Ava is super smart, and from what I've heard about you and what I know about my sister, I'd say you have a lot in common."

"How so?"

"She was obsessed with work before she came here. All business on the outside."

"And on the inside?"

"A complete romantic, who fell in love with a surfer and discovered life is more than spreadsheets. But don't tell her I said that because she still likes her spreadsheets."

"I like spreadsheets, too," he admitted.

Serena laughed. "That's what I thought. You're two peas in a pod. I barely like computers. I like living in the real world." She patted her pregnant stomach. "Although this is about to get very real, very soon, and I'm nervous about that."

"When are you due?"

"Two weeks. Maybe that's why I'm suddenly obsessed with laundry. I'm probably nesting."

"I know nothing about pregnancy, so whatever you say, I'll believe."

Her grin broadened. "You're nicer than I thought you would be... I thought you were the Big Bad Wolf who wants to blow our house down."

He did not know what to say to that, except to tell the truth. "I am here to determine whether the building should be sold. If that makes me the Big Bad Wolf, then that's what I am."

"Fair enough. Thanks again for the help."

"If you need assistance carrying this basket upstairs, let me know. I should be around, and I assume you know which apartment is mine."

"Everyone does," she said with a laugh. "But Brad or my sister should be back soon, so I won't need to bother you."

As he left the laundry room, he saw Lexie entering the courtyard, juggling a half dozen or so helium balloons in shades of pink and lavender, with a paper bag wedged under her arm, and a spool of curling ribbon tucked beneath her chin. The wind caught one balloon and nearly yanked it free. As she wrestled with it, the spool of ribbon fell to the ground, and he moved forward to grab it before it rolled into the pool.

"Thanks," she said as he put it on the table.

"Can I take the bag?"

"Would you?"

He slid it out from under her arm, and once she didn't have to worry about that, she was able to tie the balloons around the arm of a chair.

"Looks like you're having a party," he said.

"Yes. A surprise birthday party for a seven-year-old," she returned.

"That explains the seven balloons. Is this for the kid who pushed me into the pool?"

"No, it's for his best friend, a little girl named Olivia, who lives upstairs with her mother, Bree. They've had a rough few years. Olivia's father was in the military and died in a helicopter crash."

"I'm sorry to hear that."

"It was very sad. I didn't know him, but he flew with another one of our tenants, Hunter Kane. Hunter had moved in here to recover from the accident, and Bree needed a lot of help, so she dropped Olivia off one day and turned Hunter into a temporary dad. He managed to rise to the occasion with a little help from one of our other tenants, Emmalyn McGuire. Eventually, Bree came back and decided to stay here with Olivia, who was thriving with a new school, new friends, and a support system here in the building."

He smiled. "You never miss an opportunity to show off the community, do you?"

"Hey, you asked me what I was doing," she said with a shrug. "Since you're here, how about giving me a hand?"

"What about the rest of your community?" he asked dryly.

"Kaia was supposed to help, but she got called into work. Hunter and Emmalyn are keeping Bree and Olivia out of the way so we can surprise both of them. Paige and Henry are picking up the pizza, and Ava is getting the cake. I have helpers; they're just not here. But there is you..." She gave him a hopeful look.

How could he resist that? "Sure. What do you want me to do?"

"String the happy birthday sign along the fence," she said as she pulled a string of letters out of the bag. "Then I want to spread out the balloons, tie them to various chairs so that the whole area looks festive."

He took the banner. "I'll start with this."

"Great."

He smiled to himself as he took the sign over to the fence. Every time he left his apartment, he seemed to get caught up in something he hadn't expected, like working on Frank's Mustang, and now helping set up a kid's birthday party.

It took him a few moments to get the banner attached. By then, the whirlwind that was Lexie had already spread out the balloons, and covered the tables with birthday placemats, paper plates, napkins, and forks.

Serena came back into the courtyard with two presents, and they were soon joined by Margaret and Josie, who brought presents as well.

With more people to help, he was about to make his escape when Lexie called him over. "One last thing," she said. "Can you help me carry a present from my apartment out here? It's pretty heavy."

"All right. What did you get her that is so heavy?"

"It's a dollhouse. It was actually mine when I was a little girl. I had my mother ship it here so I could give it to Olivia." She led him across the courtyard. "It's quite large. My mother tended to be very extravagant with presents." She opened her unlocked door and led him into her apartment.

Lexie lived next door to her aunt on the first floor of the building, but her one-bedroom apartment was half the size of Josie's. It was also much less cluttered, with furniture in soothing tones of white, blue, and gray. But while she didn't have a lot of things, she did have a lot of photographs. There were three large, framed pictures above the couch and dozens of smaller photos covering the dining room wall.

"Did you take all these?"

"The ones over the sofa," she said as she slit open an enormous carton with a pair of scissors.

"And the ones in the dining room?" he asked, wandering over to take a closer look.

"Places I want to go. When I do, I'll replace each picture with one of my own. When the wall is completely redone, I'll feel...I don't know, like I've accomplished something."

He glanced back at her, seeing the mix of emotions in her gaze. "When are you going to start?"

"Soon. I'm saving up right now." She paused. "Could you help me pull out the dollhouse?"

He walked over as she opened the carton and, together, they extracted a large two-story dollhouse and then several ziplock bags filled with tiny furniture and people. He was impressed by the detail of not only the architecture but also the interior rooms, which had designs and even small paintings on the walls.

"This is quite a dollhouse."

"I told you. I got it on my seventh birthday, so it seems fitting I give it to Olivia."

"Are you sure you don't want to save it, maybe for one of your own kids?"

She hesitated. "I don't think so. It's beautiful, and I had fun with it, but it doesn't hold a ton of sentimental value. And to be honest, it wasn't even on my wish list that year. I wanted a robot. But my friend Melissa got a dollhouse for her birthday, which was two weeks earlier. Melissa's mother was friends with my mother, and they were always trying to outdo each other, so my mom came up with this. She won."

He smiled. "Well, at least you benefited from her competitive drive."

"I did. There were chocolate fountains at my eighth birthday tea party, pony rides for my tenth birthday, and a professional ice sculpture of me at my sweet sixteen. I was horribly embarrassed about that one. But my mother was proud as could be. If people weren't talking about one of her parties for a week, she considered it a failure."

"Was your father fully invested in your mother's party planning?"

"Not even a little bit. He was always at work. He let her do what she wanted because it kept her busy and stopped her from complaining that he was working all the time. He did get angry a few times when she really blew the budget. But she just ignored him. Impressing her friends was something she needed to do."

"Did she come from money?"

"No. Her parents, my grandparents, were teachers, so she never had parties like the ones I had, and she told me how lucky I was every time I said I wanted something simpler." Lexie shrugged. "My mother is a complicated person. I'm making her sound competitive and mercenary, but she was also generous to others. We always brought great gifts to other kids, and to be fair, I think her belief in celebrating the fun moments in life was good. Maybe she didn't have to be so extravagant, but I always felt special, and I have her to thank for that. I want Olivia to feel special, too. And I wouldn't buy this for her because that would be too much and probably make Bree feel bad. But since it's used, I feel like it will be okay." She gave him a concerned look. "You do think it will be okay, don't you?"

He nodded. "I do. Because it was yours, it will also make it more special."

"What about you? Was your mother a big party planner, too?"

"Not for me. She planned dinner parties for their friends and my father's business associates. She was groomed to be the perfect corporate wife, following in her mother's footsteps. But my birthday did not interest her. In fact, she believed that she should be getting the presents on my birthday because she went through twenty hours of labor to deliver me. Although every time she told the story, the length of time seemed to increase. I think we're up to three days of labor now," he said dryly.

"She does have a point," she said lightly.

He shook his head. "You're not taking her side."

"I just said she had a point. So, how did you celebrate your birthdays?"

"My father took my mother and me out for a very expensive dinner. She got to order whatever expensive bottle of wine or champagne she wanted, while I usually got a candle in whatever complimentary birthday dessert they served. There was never a party."

Lexie's mouth curved in both sympathy and disbelief. "That's kind of awful, Grayson."

"It wasn't that bad. And I didn't know any differently."

"But you must have gone to other kids' parties."

"Not that many. Like I said, we moved a lot, and even when we stayed in one place, we were often traveling. It wasn't like I had a crew of childhood friends."

"When is your birthday?" she asked curiously.

He gave her a pointed look. "It's not this month, I'll say that."

"I wasn't suggesting I would throw you a party."

"Not yet, you weren't, but I could see the wheels turning in your head." He cleared his throat as their gazes met and lingered for a bit too long. He really needed to stop telling her so much about himself. "Should we carry this out to the pool?"

"Yes. I'll set it up out there and put a big bow on it."

They each grabbed a side of the dollhouse and carried it out to the courtyard together. Once they'd set it up, Lexie went back to her apartment to grab all the items to put in the house, and he was about to go upstairs when he ran into Serena again, who wanted to introduce him to her husband, Brad, and her sister, Ava.

Before he knew it, he was in the center of things, hearing about Brad's bar and grill, Liam's surf school and sports chalet, and Ava's financial investing company. Ava was definitely quieter and more reserved than the others, but he could see her giving him a sharp look every now and then as if she was trying to figure him out. He still hadn't read the report she'd compiled for Lexie, who had sent it to him six months ago, and he was very afraid he was going to get called out on that. He kept wanting to slip away, but every time he tried to back out of a conversation, someone else came up and introduced themselves.

It was a happy, friendly blur of faces and smiles, all of whom were probably hoping to find a way to change his mind by welcoming him into their community. Even if their reasons for being particularly friendly to him were a little suspect, he could also see how much they genuinely cared about each other, how much they knew about each other's lives, their struggles, and their recent triumphs. It was definitely a unique environment. He couldn't remember knowing more than one or two neighbors, if that, in any of the apartment buildings he'd lived in, nor the condo tower he lived in now.

The birthday girl arrived just after noon, and after shouting "Surprise", and watching Olivia race to the dollhouse with wonder and awe in her eyes, he was introduced to more people, including Olivia's mother Bree, Hunter Kane, and Emmalyn McGuire.

One conversation led to another, and despite his efforts to extricate himself from the party, he found himself eating pizza, singing Happy Birthday, and enjoying a piece of decadent cake. As he tossed the empty plate into the trash can, he finally saw an opportunity to slip away, but the cool blonde, Ava, cut him off.

"I wanted to ask you if you'd ever read my analysis," she said.

"I did read it when I first got it, but I will take another look at it."

"If you have any questions, I'd be happy to chat with you about some of my conclusions."

"I appreciate that," he said in a neutral voice.

"But you don't really want to hear anything that will sway you from selling," she said, giving him a knowing look.

"I don't think there's anything you could say," he replied. "The land underneath this building is the most valuable part of it, and the only way to extract that value is to sell."

"You're right. But if that's what you want to do, why are you here?"

"My father asked me to spend time here before making my decision. So that's what I'm doing. Everyone has been very nice, and I appreciate the community spirit—"

"Which is, in fact, much more valuable than the land this building sits on," she said, cutting him off. "But it's an intangible, intrinsic value to those who have the good fortune to be tenants. It doesn't benefit you and your company at all. I told Lexie that when I wrote the analysis. But I also tried to show you that there are things you could do to improve profitability. Unfortunately, it's not the profitability of this building you're interested in."

"That's correct."

"I do understand, probably more than you might think. I was living in LA when my sister moved here, got a job in a bar, and then fell in love with the owner. She wanted to get married on the beach with her reception in this courtyard, and I thought she was completely out of her mind. When I came for the wedding, I felt like an outsider and also a little jealous that my sister had made so many good friends. Then she asked me to pet sit for her cat while she was on her honeymoon, and it didn't take long for me to see why this place made her so happy."

"The place or the people?"

"They go together. It's hard to explain. If you don't live here, you don't get it, so maybe it's good you're here. At least you'll know what it is you're selling. Anyway, I'm around if you ever want to talk business. I love accounting. If you want to talk numbers, I am happy to do so."

He smiled. "I also like numbers and accounting. It's very straightforward."

"If only life were the same," she said. "But I've come to appreciate the unexpected twists and turns, the intangibles, more than I ever imagined."

"Would that have something to do with your surfer guy?"

"A lot to do with Liam," she said with a laugh. "He changed my life. Anyway, if you want to escape, now's a good time." She tipped her head toward the stairs.

"I do have some work to take care of."

"Then you'd better go quickly because Josie and Margaret are setting up a card game, and if you don't leave now, you'll be here for hours."

Seeing Josie's gaze move in his direction, he knew Ava was right. "Thanks for the heads-up. I'll see you later."

He jogged up the stairs and into his apartment. As he shut the door, he felt relief at the quiet coolness of the interior, but as he sat down at his computer, his mind kept drifting not just to the party below, but also to the people who had gathered to make one little girl feel like the most special person on the planet. The tenants did seem to go out of their way for each other.

He told himself it didn't matter. Even if he didn't sell, it wouldn't always be this way, this same group of people. It was an apartment building. Serena and Brad were having a kid. They might decide they need a house one day. Same with Madison and Gabe, and Ava and Liam. People would come and go. The community would change. He was just going to force it to change a little sooner.

As he flipped through the files on his computer, he came across Ava's report and thought about reading through it, but what was the point? He wasn't going to change his mind. The value of the building was in the land, not the people. And he was a businessman. It was his job to make money for the company, for the employees they supported, and for their investors.

With that reminder, he skipped over the report and moved on to the business he could actually close in the next few days, a sale that didn't involve anyone he knew, which certainly made things a lot easier.

CHAPTER SEVEN

Wednesday morning, Lexie walked into town, relieved to have some time for herself. She'd spent the first two days of the week at a series of family and engagement photo shoots, as well as taking several meetings with prospective brides. She'd also spent several hours yesterday trying to get the perfect shot of Maeve Rian's poodle—an exhausting test of patience that only reinforced her doubts about the new career path she had created for herself.

She'd never wanted a career shooting brides, families, and pets, but those photo shoots were taking up most of her time, and she had little left to pursue her real goals. Maybe Grayson had been somewhat right when he'd suggested she'd traded one form of servitude for another, and one that also paid less.

It was time to start changing her priorities. She'd left her law job more than two years ago, and she hadn't replaced one photo on her dining room wall. She had to do better, and the first step was talking to the gallery owner to see if she could still set up a show. Having a deadline might force her to get her act together.

A few minutes later, she stopped in front of an art gallery on Fourth Avenue. Taking a breath to strengthen her resolve, she opened the door, a small brass bell emitting a soft, cheerful chime as she stepped inside, the cool air a welcome break from the rising heat outside.

The Art Nest was quiet at mid-morning, sunlight pouring through tall front windows and spilling across polished hardwood floors. Framed photographs and paintings covered the walls—seascapes, abstracts, portraits—the best of local talent curated with Sienna Dunne's impeccable eye. Sienna, a dark-eyed brunette in her early thirties, gave her a smile as she moved from behind the front counter to greet her.

"Lexie. It's good to see you. I hope you're here to tell me you want to take me up on my offer."

"I do." She still felt uncertain about that decision, but the words had already left her mouth. "If you're still interested."

"Of course. I would love to have you show during the art walk on the Fourth of July weekend."

That was almost three months away, which gave her the time she needed. "That would be perfect because I want to work on getting more shots before then."

"Great. Let's put you on the calendar for July first through the end of the month. If things go well, we'll do another show in the fall."

"I hope it goes well. I'm nervous about it."

Sienna gave her a warm smile. "Every artist says exactly the same thing to me, and I understand, but I also know talent when I see it. And I've seen it in some of the photos you showed me a few weeks ago. I'm glad you decided to move forward."

"You're handing me a great opportunity. I don't know why I even hesitated. Thank you, Sienna. I hope I won't let you down."

"You won't." As another customer entered the gallery, she said goodbye and headed outside, feeling both exhilarated and terrified. She'd taken the first step, but there was still a long way to go before she'd be ready for a show. And she needed coffee to think about what to do next.

She'd only gone half a block when she saw Grayson standing in front of the hardware store, phone in hand, his brow furrowed like the screen had personally insulted him. Wearing dark jeans, a white shirt with sleeves rolled to the elbows, and expensive sunglasses, he looked handsome and sophisticated, and a tingle ran down her spine. When she hadn't been thinking about her business goals, she'd been thinking about him, wondering what he'd been doing, because she hadn't seen him at all. If she hadn't seen his car in the lot, she might have thought he'd decided to bail on his month at Ocean Shores. But apparently not...

"Grayson?" she said. "Are you lost?"

His head whipped up, a frown crossing his lips. "I'm looking for a print shop. It's supposed to be nearby, but my GPS sent me here."

"I know where the shop is. It's tucked on a side street around the corner, and GPS often doesn't find shops on that street. You're close. I can show you if you want."

"Thanks. What are you up to?" he asked as they walked down the block.

"I just stopped in at the gallery that's interested in giving me a show."

He gave her a questioning look. "And..."

"I told her I'd like to do it. Thankfully, the owner wants to schedule my show for early July, so I have time to get more photos, which I definitely need to do."

"How do you feel?"

"Excited. Scared out of my mind. Afraid I won't be able to come up with work that I'm really proud of. Which is probably more than you wanted to know."

"It sounds like you have time to make it happen the way you want to."

"I have a few months. However, a lot of my time is filled with events I've already committed to. But I'll just have to work harder. Anyway, what have you been doing this week? I haven't seen you since Olivia's birthday party."

"I've been working on a development deal in Singapore."

"Singapore, wow. That's interesting."

"It is, but it's also complicated. I'm picking up some blueprints now."

"Have you been to Singapore?"

"Several times. It's a beautiful country. And this building will be a work of art. We have an incredible architect lined up. Unfortunately, we're running into unexpected obstacles, so it's still not a done deal."

"Are you tearing something else down to build this work of art?"

"Yes, that's usually how it works. But the building has been abandoned. It's not in good shape."

"So, no one lives there?"

"No."

She nodded, although she suspected her building wasn't the first one to be bought and sold by his company, with people displaced, lives shattered. She couldn't imagine doing a job like that.

"You shouldn't judge what you don't know," Grayson said, giving her a pointed look.

She met his gaze. "How do you know what I'm thinking?"

"Because you have a very expressive face, and you show your emotions."

"I just don't see how it could possibly feel good to kick people out of their homes."

"You're making it too personal."

"What you're doing at Ocean Shores is personal to me."

"We don't kick people out into the cold. We give them relocation packages, which is more than a lot of companies do. When you're a renter, your home is always going to be dependent on what the owner wants. If you really want security, you have to own your own place."

"I know that, but not everyone can afford to own."

"I understand, but that's not on me or my company."

"Let's not talk about this," she said. "I was in a good mood, and I'd like to stay that way a while longer."

"Fine with me," he said as they turned the corner.

They walked halfway down the block to the print shop. "Here it is," she said.

"Thanks." He paused. "This should only take a moment. Do you want to get coffee or something to celebrate your gallery decision?"

She hesitated, knowing that spending more time with this frustrating man was probably a bad idea, but she still didn't want to say no. "I was planning to get some coffee."

"Do you mind if I join you?"

She was surprised he wanted to join her after the little argument they'd just had, but she needed to keep talking to him. It was the only way to fight. "Of course not. I'd love the company."

She followed Grayson into the print shop, and within minutes, he'd picked up a cardboard tube that contained blueprints, and then they headed out of the building.

The coffee shop was just around the corner. Since it was late for breakfast and early for lunch, the café was fairly empty. They picked up coffees at the counter and then found a table by the window, sunlight spilling across the worn wood, the hum of conversation from three older ladies blending with the hiss of the espresso machine.

"What else is on your agenda today?" Grayson asked as they settled into their seats.

"Planning out the photographs I need to make my collection sing."

"What's at the top of the list?"

"I heard about some caves about five miles south of here that are only accessible during very low tides, which happens a half dozen times a year. Apparently, someone once died when they stayed too long and didn't get out before the water rushed back in."

"Sounds dangerous."

"But doesn't it sound like I could get some great pictures?"

"Yes," he admitted. "Will there be any low tides coming up?"

"There's actually one on Saturday morning. The tide will be at its lowest point in the past three months at seven a.m. I'd probably have an hour to get in and out."

"I don't think you should go alone. What if you run into problems?"

"If I run into problems, I wouldn't want to risk anyone else's life."

"This is sounding less and less like a good idea," he said with a frown.

"I don't think it's that dangerous as long as I move quickly. And this is what I wanted to do when I quit my law job. I wanted to take chances and explore and show the world to people who don't have the time or money to see it for themselves." She paused. "I'm going to do it. I'm going to finally stop making excuses and just go. And I can't die—I have a wedding to shoot at three thirty on Saturday afternoon."

Concern filled his gaze. "I don't know, Lexie. It sounds risky."

"Isn't everything worth doing a little risky? It's rumored that the caves were once used for smuggling. Who knows what I might find inside? Maybe some old gold coins."

"Or maybe some bones," he said darkly.

She shivered at that. "Stop trying to scare me, Grayson."

"I think you should be scared."

"I am a little," she admitted. "But I shouldn't let fear stop me, right?"

"I'm coming with you."

Surprise ran through her at his declaration. "No way you're coming with me."

"Why not?"

"Well...I don't know. Why would you want to?"

"I don't think you should go alone, and if you don't want to ask your friends, then I'll go."

"You just said it was risky."

"And you just reminded me that there's little reward without risk."

She stared at him for a long minute, not quite sure why he'd made the offer, but she was going to accept before he changed his mind. "Okay. But if we find any gold coins, they're mine. You're already rich."

His smile parted his lips. "I say we split any reward. I'm not going treasure hunting without a stake in the find."

"We're not treasure hunting. I'm going to take photographs."

"Well, I'm going to look for treasure, because I can't imagine a better place to find something unexpected."

"You look way too excited now for someone who just said this was dangerous," she said with a smile.

"I still think it's dangerous, but I have to admit that it also sounds exciting."

She thought so, too, but it wasn't just the idea of exploring the caves that was exciting her— it was spending more time with him.

―――

Saturday morning, Grayson checked his watch as he parked at the end of a dirt road that led to an overgrown hiking trail. It was six-fifteen in the morning, and the sky was just beginning to lighten with the first hints of dawn. Lexie had been quiet since they'd left Ocean Shores, and he didn't know if the past twenty minutes of silence was because she was still half asleep, was worrying about going into the caves, or had something to do with him.

"Are you sure this is the right place?" he asked, peering through the windshield at the steep, rocky coastline that dropped precipitously to the beach, the vast ocean waves crashing onto the jagged rocks below with an intimidating force.

"According to the GPS, it is. The water looks like it's high."

"Hard to tell from here. We need to get closer." He gave her a look. "You don't have to do this if you're having second thoughts. I won't judge you."

"I'll judge myself if I back out before even giving it a try."

"Well, you can still change your mind at any point."

"I know," she said with a determined nod. "But for now, I'm going."

"And I'm going with you."

As they got out of the car, she grabbed her camera bag and hung it over one shoulder, with another camera hanging from a strap around her neck. "Two cameras?" he asked in surprise.

"One for digital, one for film. I doubt I'll ever do this again, so I want to cover all my bases."

"I'm curious. Did you take classes in photography or are you self-taught?" he asked as they headed down a dirt path.

"I took several classes because that's what I do when I'm interested in something. I research everything I can about it."

He bit back a smile, thinking that was something else they had in common, although he'd never wanted to know anything about photography. But he had a feeling he was going to learn a lot more about it in the next hour.

They made their way down the trail, which became more treacherous the closer they got to the beach. It was steep in places, with loose rocks and slippery dirt, which was probably slick from the constant spray of the ocean.

Lexie was ahead of him, but he stayed as close as he could as they slipped and slid a few times, reaching out to each other to steady themselves. When they finally made it to the sand, the ocean was receding, leaving about eight feet of wet, sandy beach between the ocean and a jagged rocky, cliff with narrow openings that led into the caves. Despite the outgoing tide, the waves still sent water back up the beach a little too close for his comfort, making him wonder what the hell he was doing.

He wasn't an adventurer or an explorer. He was good at boardroom negotiations, at selling, making money, growing a business, and none of that had left time for impulsive adventures like this.

As Lexie glanced back at him, he saw the same uncertainty in her gaze.

"Maybe this is a bad idea," she said.

"It could be," he admitted. "But..."

"But it could be amazing, and we're here, so we should do it, right?" she finished.

Her worried gaze clung to his, and despite his misgivings, he felt a compelling need to help her do what she'd come here to do. "Yes, we should do it."

The grateful smile she gave him warmed his entire soul. "Thank you, Grayson."

"Thank me when this is over."

Lexie glanced at her watch. "The tide should be out for another fifty-five minutes."

"Let's aim to be in and out in forty," he said, "so we have a fifteen-minute buffer. I'll set my alarm and keep us on track. I want you to focus on getting your photographs without worrying about the time."

"I appreciate that." She drew in a deep breath. "Let's go."

"After you."

Lexie jumped onto the sand and led the way toward the largest open crevice. Before entering, she pulled a beanie from her bag. It had a light attached to the front. She slipped it over her head, then turned on the beam, flashing it over the rocky walls. He stayed close to her back as they stepped inside. The air smelled of salt and seaweed, with an underlying hint of something more mysterious—the scent of dark, hidden places that were never completely dry.

"It's incredible," Lexie breathed, immediately pulling out her camera and adjusting the settings for the low light.

"And a little spooky," he muttered.

"That's true, but that's part of the experience. Look at how the rocks have been shaped and carved by the water that goes in and out." She started snapping photos while he turned on the flashlight on his phone as she moved deeper into the chamber.

"Don't go too far," he said.

"We have time," she said, continuing forward.

He knew they had time, but he felt reluctant to leave the entranceway. He'd never had a problem with claustrophobia, but he'd never been in a cave before. As he took a few more steps in her direction, he flashed his light off the walls, pausing when he saw a heart scratched into the rocks. "Look at this," he said.

She came back, snapping her camera at the heart, the initials that appeared to be a J and maybe an A or an E, but he couldn't quite tell.

"I wonder who they were," she said, tracing the initials with her finger. "And how long ago they were here. I wished they'd scratched out a date. It could be an interesting love story."

He smiled as her imagination took flight. "You're already making one up in your head, aren't you? It was probably just a couple of bored teenagers."

"Maybe."

"We'll never know." He checked his watch. "And we have got thirty-five minutes now. Let's keep going."

They moved down a narrow path, which suddenly widened into a chamber, perhaps fifteen feet wide and twenty feet deep. The floor was a mix of sand and stones, with occasional pools of seawater swirling in deeper depressions. The light grew brighter, too, and as they looked up, he saw cracks in the rocks where the morning sun was beaming through, adding a different kind of mysterious beauty to the location.

"Oh my God," Lexie whispered, her voice echoing slightly in the enclosed space. "This is amazing. There are so many details to see, all of them created by nature, by the sea."

She was right. In some places, the rock had been worn so smooth it looked like polished marble. In others, it maintained a rough, organic texture that spoke of violent storms and crashing waves.

"Look at this," Lexie said, pointing to a section of wall where the rock had been worn into what looked almost like a spiral staircase, though one meant for giants rather than humans.

The light from above created an almost cathedral-like atmosphere, and Lexie immediately began shooting photo after photo, adjusting her settings, her light, moving around to find the perfect angle, switching between digital and film.

As she lost herself in her passionate quest to find the right shot, the best detail, he checked his watch again. Another ten minutes had flown by. They had twenty-five minutes to go. He wanted to shout out the time, but her focus and concentration were on what she'd come to do, and he didn't want to get in the way. He poked around a side path, wondering if it led into another cave, and saw that it ended with a smaller chamber.

Lexie caught up with him as he pressed forward, passing him by to see what was ahead. This smaller area was cooler and slightly darker, but something shiny caught his gaze, and he swung his light in that direction.

"Lexie," he said. "Look. Is that gold?"

"Seriously? You found a gold coin?"

"I don't think it's a coin." He pointed his light at a gold chain caught in a crevice in the rocky wall.

Lexie moved forward. "It's a necklace," she said, pausing to snap a few more photos before pulling the chain off a sharp, jagged piece of stone. "A locket," she said, holding it up to him. "Maybe it belonged to whoever carved their initials in the rocks."

"Or someone else," he said. "I'm sure many people have explored this cave over the years."

"It looks old." She struggled to open the gold locket, finally managing to flip it open. "There's a picture, but it has faded from the water and the air."

She handed it to him, and he took a look at the picture, not able to make out the features of the woman's face, but the locket still felt like a tangible connection to another time, another person who had been in this cave. "I hope this didn't belong to the person who died here."

Lexie frowned. "That's a morbid thought."

"You're the one who told me the story."

"Yes, but now I don't want to think about that. And I don't want to believe whoever owned this locket died here. I prefer to believe the locket fell off, and she lost it."

"It does look like the clasp is broken," he said, handing it back to her.

She slipped it into her pocket. "We'll take another look when we have better light."

"I'm going to check on the water level. Why don't you come back into the bigger chamber? The light is better there."

"I agree."

He was relieved when she followed him because he didn't want to find anything in the darker portion of the cave that would change the tone of their adventure.

She took more angled shots of the light coming in from above, bouncing off the rocks with a shimmer. He moved toward the opening of the caves, pausing near the front to check the tide. It was definitely starting to come back in, but they still had some time.

As he turned back, he saw Lexie pointing her camera at him.

"What are you doing?"

"Shooting pictures of you," she said as she kept snapping.

"I'm not a wonder of nature."

"The light caught your silhouette in the most amazing way," she said. "I couldn't resist."

He checked his watch again. "We have fifteen minutes. Don't waste them on me."

She moved back into the deeper part of the cave, squatting down next to an unexpected patch of grass that was growing through part of the rock wall. The fact that she'd even noticed that small detail impressed him. In fact, watching her work was one surprise after another—her ability to see beauty in rough textures and shadows, the way she crouched to capture angles he never would have considered, how she found art in the smallest details. He found himself completely mesmerized by her actions. She looked beyond the obvious, searching for the unusual, for the contradiction.

As a gust of wind lifted his hair and brushed his face, his attention was drawn back to the opening of the cave. When he moved toward the entrance, the breeze threw a watery spray into his face. The ocean was getting closer. He checked his watch. They had ten minutes before his safe-zone time ended, but he was starting to worry. The wind was blowing hard, and that made the inrushing sea look a lot more threatening.

"Lexie, we should go."

"You said we had fifteen minutes."

"That was five minutes ago. But the tide is coming in faster than I expected, and the waves are getting bigger."

"Almost done," she promised as she clicked another three times in rapid succession. "The light is perfect now." She swung the camera back in his direction, taking several more photos before he realized he was the focus once more.

"I told you I'm not your model."

"It's the perfect contrast—man against nature. I can see the water behind you now."

"Exactly. It's getting too close. Let's get out of here."

"All right."

She reluctantly followed him to the entrance, gasping when a wave larger than the others sent water rushing toward their feet. "It's too soon," she said in surprise. "The tidal charts said we'd have an hour, and it hasn't even been forty minutes."

"I don't think the ocean cares about charts," he said, grabbing her hand as he pulled her away from the entrance to the cave. They still had to get across the wet sand and up the slippery, steep slope that was getting wetter by the minute.

They ran toward the path, getting caught by another swirling pool of water that soaked their shoes and ankles, which made it even more difficult to get up the first part of the hill. He'd only taken a few steps when Lexie slipped, almost pulling him down with her, but he hung tightly to her hand.

She gave him a terrified look. "I'm not sure I can make it up this hill in time."

"You can. *We can*," he said forcefully. "We have to. I want to see what photos you took, and the world needs to see them, too."

She gave him a determined nod and tried to find a drier, rockier place to put her foot. It wasn't easy. Every incoming wave sent seawater flowing over the rocks and the hillside, and it took all his strength and hers for them to stay together, to keep moving upward. They were about halfway when she paused to catch her breath, and they both made the mistake of looking behind them.

"Oh, my God! The ocean is in the cave," she murmured. "Another few minutes..."

"Come on. We have to keep going."

The second half of their journey was as harrowing as the first part, the wind throwing water not only on the rocks but also on them. Finally, they climbed back onto the flat land at the top of the bluff.

"We made it," Lexie said, breathing hard.

"We did." Even though they'd only climbed a hillside about thirty feet high, he felt like they'd made it to the top of a mountain. For a long moment, they just looked at each other, the intensity of what they'd just shared hanging between them. Her hair had escaped its ponytail in damp, curly strands, and there was something wild and alive in her expression that took his breath away.

"That was scary," she said. "But also exciting."

The sun caught her flushed face, and she was practically glowing with exhilaration. She was beautiful and completely alive, and before he could think about what he was doing, he cupped her face in his hands and kissed her warm, salty lips, feeling a passionate fever that seemed to be consuming her as much as it was consuming him. He didn't know how long they stood on the bluff and kissed, but it felt far too short. When a gusty wind doused them with another ocean spray, they broke apart with a breathless laugh.

"That was..." Lexie began, then trailed off, her fingers touching her lips.

"Yeah," he agreed, his gaze meeting hers. "It was."

As she turned away from him and looked back at the ocean, he put his arm around her shoulders. Then they watched the tide continue its relentless advance until the water flowing into the caves was at the top of the crevice.

"It's hard to believe now we were in there," she murmured.

"I'm glad we're out."

She turned back to face him. "Thank you, Grayson. For coming with me, for watching the time, for helping me up the hill, and for not letting me fall into the sea and drown..."

"You're more than welcome. Although some of that was for me, too," he said dryly.

"I get a little distracted when I'm taking photos. If I'd been alone—"

"Which you weren't. And to be honest, I'm glad I came, because this was...an experience," he said, knowing he would never forget it. And for that, he should probably be thanking her. As she shivered, he added, "Let's go home."

As they headed to the car, he was struck by the fact that he'd just thought of Ocean Shores as home, and that might be the most terrifying thought he'd had all day.

CHAPTER EIGHT

Three hours later, Lexie couldn't stop thinking about her early morning adventure with Grayson, and it wasn't just the cave exploration that ran through her mind but also the crazy, passionate kisses they'd shared when they'd gotten to the top of the bluff. That had been a completely unexpected and shockingly good moment. The man she'd considered her worst enemy was not only very attractive, but he also kissed like a dream. Besides that, she couldn't forget how carefully he'd kept watch over both of them and how tightly he'd held her hand when she'd almost slipped down the wet rocks. She couldn't have picked a better person to go with her.

When they'd arrived back at Ocean Shores, Grayson had muttered something about having work to do, and they'd parted with a few simple words about having fun that hadn't begun to cover the experience they'd shared.

As soon as she'd gotten into her apartment, she'd spent a good twenty minutes in a hot shower before dressing and making breakfast. Then she'd started developing her film in her makeshift darkroom, formerly her walk-in closet.

The darkroom reminded her of the cave—minus the scent of sea and salt, replaced instead with the acrid bite of chemicals.

She moved between the enlarger and the chemical bath, watching her photographs slowly materialize like magic.

The film captured details and tones that made her breath catch. The natural spotlight streaming down from the cave's ceiling had created the most incredible contrast, and the texture of the ancient rock walls seemed to leap off the photographic paper.

And then there were the shots of Grayson.

She hadn't expected them to turn out so well. The way the light had caught him, turning him from a rigid businessman into something almost mythical—a figure carved from the same stone as the cave itself. He'd been completely transformed. And in one frame, he was looking up toward the cave's ceiling, his expression unguarded, almost reverent. In another, he was reaching toward her, concern evident in every line of his body as he'd urged her to hurry.

They were some of the best portraits she'd ever done.

The ring of her bell caught her attention. She slid past the heavy, dark curtain she'd put in front of the door to block any light when she left the closet and moved through her living room.

A knock came at her door, followed by her aunt's voice. "Lexie? Are you home?"

"Coming," she called, throwing open the door.

Josie walked into her apartment wearing a flowing purple floral dress and her signature collection of silver bracelets, her red hair pulled back with a butterfly clip. "How was the cave? I'm dying to hear what you thought."

"It was spectacular," she said. "More than I imagined it would be."

"I knew you would love it," Josie said with an approving smile. "I'm glad you made the time to go."

"How did you know I would love it?" she asked, curious about her aunt's choice of words. "Have you been in those caves?

Because when I talked about them before, you never said anything about being there."

"I thought I had." She shrugged. "It was many, many years ago. I'm glad they were still accessible."

"They were, but barely. The time we had was shorter than I'd anticipated. Luckily, Grayson was keeping track of the time."

"Yes, Grayson." Her aunt's eyes took on a new light. "I was surprised when you texted me last night and said you were going with him. How on earth did that happen?"

"I ran into him in town a few days ago and mentioned the caves, and he offered to come along."

"That seems out of character. I thought he was all business all the time."

"So did I. It turns out he has an adventurous side. I was very glad he was there, because it would have been terrifying to go in alone. But you probably know that, since you've been there."

"I remember it being thrilling, but I also remember the tide being out for a couple of hours, so it felt exciting but not that dangerous. I guess the tides have changed over the years. Did you get some good photos?"

"Tons." She walked over to her dining room table to turn on her computer. "Here are a few of the digital shots. I'm developing the film now."

Josie settled into the chair in front of the computer as the digital images filled the screen. The cave shots were stunning even on the monitor—the otherworldly beauty of the hidden chamber, the interplay of natural light and shadow, the sense of ancient mystery. And for a few minutes, they were both quiet as she scrolled from one shot to the next.

"Oh, my," Josie breathed. "Lexie, these are extraordinary."

"I know," she said, unable to hide her excitement. "This is the kind of photography I've always wanted to do." She clicked through several more images, pausing on the shot of Grayson silhouetted in the entrance to the cave. "He didn't like it when I took his picture, but the way he looked—it was impossible to resist. He looks like he's one with nature, don't you think? It's not the way I thought of him before."

"He's a very handsome man," Josie observed. "It sounds like you may have changed your mind about him."

"Not completely. I know he still wants to sell the building, but that wasn't on my mind when I was taking his picture. He didn't feel like my enemy, more like my friend. Which is not even true. I mean, we're not friends."

"What are you then?" Josie asked with a mischievous smile. "More than friends?"

"I didn't mean it like that," she said, feeling her cheeks warm.

"Something happened."

"Nothing happened," she lied. "We explored the caves. He made sure we got out before the ocean swallowed us up, and it was nice to have him there. That's all."

"Okay, well, I'm glad."

"Why are you glad?" she asked, feeling a bit confused. "Do you want me to like Grayson? Because it doesn't seem like you should want that when he's threatening to take away our homes, and you've lived here for more than thirty years."

"I understand his position, and I'm still hoping he changes his mind. But I don't need you to hate him. What will be will be. I'm just happy you had fun and that you got a chance to do what you've been wanting to do for a while. I was beginning to worry you were getting too entrenched in your wedding photos."

She started at the word wedding. "Speaking of which..." She checked her watch, relieved she still had two hours before she had to leave. "I have a wedding to do this afternoon. I need to finish developing my film."

"I'll let you go then."

She closed her computer, and as Josie stood up, her gaze caught on the locket that was lying on the table. It had been hidden from view when the monitor was open.

Josie sucked in a quick gulp of air. "Where did you get that?"

"It's the most amazing story. I found it in the cave, tucked in between some rocks." She picked up the locket and opened it. "The picture is too faded to see who it is, unfortunately. I looked for an inscription, but I didn't see one. I wish I could return it to its owner, but I have no idea how to find that person. It could have been in the cave for years."

"That's exactly where it's been," Josie murmured, extending her hand, her eyes suddenly bright and a little watery.

"Aunt Josie?" she asked as she put the locket in her hand. "Have you seen this before?"

"Yes, I have," she said, her voice soft and breathy, filled with emotion. "It's mine, Lexie."

"No way," she breathed. "It's yours? How is that possible?"

"I thought I'd lost it in my apartment or that it had fallen off at some point as I was walking around town. But, of course, it was in the cave."

"The picture inside the locket is you?"

"It was me, but it's been erased." Her aunt shook her head as she stared down at the open locket, at the faded picture. "It makes sense that the image is gone because I haven't been that girl in a long time."

She waited, sensing her aunt wanted to say more.

Finally, she did. "I used to go to that beach often, to that wild, desolate bluff. The waves crashing on the rocks often suited my mood, which was turbulent at times. I had decisions to make, and I wasn't sure which path to take, which choice to make. When the tide was out, I would go into the cave. I liked the darkness, the mystery, the feeling that some things last forever, that they can't be broken by constant waves of pressure and change. It felt like a metaphor for my life."

"Was this when you were deciding whether you wanted to go back to acting?"

"That was one of my decisions, yes, but it was more than that. I didn't just quit acting because I'd stopped liking it. I was hurt—deeply hurt. I'd been betrayed by people I trusted, people I loved, and they were all wrapped up in the acting world. I had to leave everything behind to find my soul again, and, eventually, I did."

"Did someone give you the locket?"

"Yes." Josie smiled to herself, not looking sad anymore.

"Who was it?"

"It doesn't matter. Do you mind if I keep this?"

"Of course not. It's yours. I'm just glad I found it."

"Me, too. I should let you go."

"Aunt Josie," she said. "I feel like there's more to this story than what you're telling me."

Her aunt simply smiled and said, "I suppose there is, but now isn't the time to tell that story. Maybe one day." She put her hand on Lexie's shoulder. "I'm happy you brought this back to me, but I'm even happier about the photos you took today and the smile I see on your face now. I feel like you're becoming the woman you want to be."

"Perhaps a little too slowly, but this was a good day," she admitted. "I'm going to start making more changes in my life, start going after what I really want." She paused, wanting to make one thing clear. "But that doesn't mean I'm giving up the fight to keep this building. That's still at the top of the list."

"Along with Grayson."

She frowned. "Well, yes, because he's the one on the other side of this fight."

"I don't think that's the only reason he's on your mind," Josie said as she moved to the door.

"It is," she told her, but her aunt just gave her a wave and shut the door behind her. "It is," she repeated, but she wasn't sure she believed that any more than Josie did.

Saturday night, Grayson made the forty-minute drive from Oceanside to San Diego to meet with a real estate developer who might be interested in the Ocean Shores property. As he walked into Pendry's rooftop bar, he felt immediately at home. It was the kind of bar he often frequented—sleek, modern, expensive, and filled with dealmakers.

Jeff Parrish was waiting at a corner table, a man in his early forties with perfectly styled dark hair and the confident smile of someone who'd built a fortune by moving fast and taking big risks. Jeff's company was headquartered in Los Angeles, but he was down in San Diego for a few days and had asked to meet him for a drink to discuss the Ocean Shores property.

"Grayson!" Jeff stood, extending a hand. "I'm glad you could make it."

"I was surprised to hear you were in San Diego."

"Drove down today. Doing a walk-through of one of our properties tomorrow. I thought we could discuss your beachfront building."

"Of course," he said, settling into his chair.

"Let's have a drink before we get into it." Jeff flagged down a waitress, a pretty blonde in her twenties. "Another Scotch for me, and whatever my friend here is drinking."

"I'll have the same," he said, watching Jeff's gaze follow the waitress back to the bar.

"Nice," Jeff said, a gleam in his eyes.

He smiled. Jeff was not only a big-time investor; he was also a big-time player. "Aren't you seeing someone?"

"I'm always seeing someone," Jeff said with a careless laugh. "What about you?"

"Too busy with work."

"And when you're not working..."

He shrugged. "That doesn't happen often."

"I'm all for focusing on business, but you have to make time for fun, too, Grayson. Spend some of that money you're making and blow off some steam."

"I've been having fun."

"When?" Jeff challenged.

"Actually, this morning. I explored an ocean cave when the

tide went out and allowed us to gain access for a short time. It was very cool."

"You went into a dark cave that you could have died in, and that was fun?" Jeff asked with disbelief. "Tell me there was a pretty woman involved."

"There might have been," he admitted.

Jeff gave him a knowing look. "Now, we're getting to the fun part. I've never done it in a cave."

He rolled his eyes, seeing the glint in Jeff's eyes. "It wasn't like that."

"Why the hell not? That could have been a once-in-a-lifetime experience. Who's the woman?"

"No one you know," he said vaguely, relieved when the waitress brought their drinks. "Shall we get down to business?"

"Sure."

Jeff pulled out the folder he'd sent him on the property, and for the next hour, they discussed square footage, zoning regulations, and potential profit margins. Jeff's vision for the property was ambitious—luxury condominiums starting at two million, with penthouses going for considerably more.

"The location isn't as luxurious as I would like," Jeff said. "But I'm thinking we could buy up a smaller property just down the block and put in a spa, maybe some pickleball courts. That seems to be all the rage."

"That's true."

"And there's a country club golf course only five miles away. Maybe we can add in a membership as a perk. We'll have buyers lined up before we break ground," Jeff added. "Right now, you have eighteen units bringing in what, maybe, thirty thousand a month total? This new property would generate ten times that amount." He leaned back, clearly energized by the numbers. "This is exactly the kind of deal that gets my blood pumping."

Grayson nodded, recognizing the familiar excitement in Jeff's voice. He'd felt that same rush countless times before, the intoxicating prospect of turning a good investment into a great one.

But tonight, something felt different. The numbers were impressive, the potential enormous, but the thrill wasn't quite there. And he was blaming that lack of excitement directly on Lexie.

She'd gotten into his head. She was making him think about all the people who would be losing their homes instead of all the possibilities. But those possibilities weren't for Lexie or the other tenants. They'd be given relocation packages that would allow them to rent other apartments in the area, but they would never be able to go back to Ocean Shores. Shaking his head, he reminded himself he was being too sentimental. And that had never been one of his weaknesses.

"What's the timeline?" Jeff asked.

"I need to finish my evaluation. Another few weeks."

"Why so long? Is something going on?"

"No. I just have things to take care of before we can entertain offers."

"Don't wait too long," Jeff warned, signaling the waitress for another round. "When opportunity knocks, you answer, and that opportunity is practically knocking down your door."

"I'm aware."

"Good. Glad to hear it. Now, tell me more about the woman who took you into a cave."

"Nothing to tell. She's a photographer, and she was taking pictures. I was just checking out the cave."

"Does Victoria Sterling know you're exploring caves with someone else? My sister is friends with her. She said Victoria has been talking a lot about you."

"We've only gone out a few times. It's nothing," he said with a shrug.

"Better make sure she knows that. I grew up with girls like Victoria. She's nearing thirty, her friends are all married, and she's getting itchy. That's why I don't date anyone over twenty-seven anymore." Jeff gave a hearty laugh, but there was also something hollow about it.

Jeff was ten years his senior and chasing women far younger

than him. It should have seemed enviable—the freedom, the wealth, the endless options, a new beautiful woman every weekend, but it just seemed...lonely.

The waitress brought them another round of drinks, and Jeff raised his glass. "To working together. To our generation making things even bigger and better than they've been."

He clinked his glass, sipped his Scotch, and felt far too eager to end the meeting. And as their conversation moved to golf, Jeff's third favorite topic after business and women, he wished he could find an excuse to leave.

As if on cue, he got a text. It was from Victoria.

The Children's Hospital gala is next Saturday. Should I put you down as my plus-one? It's the social event of the season. Let me know ASAP. The tables are filling up fast.

He stared at the message, feeling a distinct lack of interest in her text, too. What was wrong with him? Golf and society events were as much a part of his life as Jeff's. But right now, that life felt very far away. And Jeff had just reminded him that women like Victoria didn't like casual relationships that weren't going anywhere.

"Problem?" Jeff asked.

"Yes," he said, seeing his opportunity to go. "There's an issue with a deal I'm doing in Singapore. I have to make a call. But this has been good. I'll be in touch."

"I hope to hear from you soon."

He nodded, took another sip of his scotch and then got up and left. Jeff called the waitress over as he walked away, and when he got to the door, he looked back and saw them chatting. Jeff really didn't waste an opportunity when he saw one.

But he was more than happy to go. He was tired and feeling off. He needed a good night's sleep. Then he'd start feeling more like himself again. But as he neared Ocean Shores, he thought about Jeff's plans to turn the complex into a luxury condo building, to create a spa nearby, perhaps with pickleball courts, and other entertainment opportunities. This whole area would look completely different. It wouldn't be a neighborhood for the average person, someone working a blue-collar job like Kaia or Ben, or building their own businesses, like Lexie, Ava, Liam, Madison, and Gabe.

That wasn't his problem, he reminded himself. Change always came. Progress couldn't be stopped.

But it wasn't just thinking about Ocean Shores that had made him feel restless; it was seeing Jeff, hearing him talk about their shared world. Did he want to follow the same path as Jeff? Did he want to be chasing deals and younger women when he was forty-three? He'd never thought much about marriage or family. He hadn't seen a loving marriage between his parents, and it was the excitement of eventually running his father's company that had always gotten him up in the morning.

With a sigh, he pulled into the parking lot just after eight. He could hear the soft murmur of conversation and laughter as soon as he walked into the courtyard. Lexie was sitting on the other side of the pool at a table with Kaia and Emmalyn, a bottle of wine between them, the string lights over the pool casting a warm glow over their faces.

He paused in the shadows, knowing they'd invite him to join them as soon as they saw him. But that would be a mistake. He'd already gotten too close to Lexie. The cave experience and the kisses that had followed had been damned good. Too good. Too memorable. Which was why he was going into his apartment and locking the door, not to keep anyone out, but to keep himself in.

CHAPTER NINE

Lexie spent most of Sunday going through her photos. They were the best photographs she'd ever taken—leaving her proud but also annoyed it had taken her so long to push herself.

As she looked back at her life since leaving her father's law firm, she saw how one day of busywork had led to the next, how she'd gotten caught up in helping her aunt, then in all the side jobs to bring in money. She'd been memorializing the most important moments of other people's lives, but she hadn't been living her own life.

But yesterday, that had changed. Going into that cave had freed her from all the restrictions she'd placed on herself, and she was never going to be the same woman she was. And she had Grayson to thank for giving her the impetus to change things up, to have a thrilling adventure, to push herself in a way she never had before. It was an experience she would never forget. Nor would she forget the kisses they'd shared. Because she had a feeling that wasn't going to happen again.

Grayson hadn't talked to her since they'd gotten back yesterday morning, and she'd seen him slip up to his apartment last night without coming over to say hello, which meant he hadn't wanted to talk to her, which was a little disappointing.

While she might normally respect his desire for space, she couldn't let him have too much space, because she still had to stop him from selling. She had to keep trying to bring him into the group, even if he didn't really want to. She might need some help to do that. And as she walked out of her apartment around four, she found just the people she was looking for.

Emmalyn and Hunter were sitting at the pool as Olivia and Henry swam nearby. She sat down on the lounger next to Emmalyn. "Are you two babysitting?"

"Yes," Emmalyn replied. "Paige and Bree are getting their nails done. They needed some no-kid time, and neither one of them can join us for girls' night at Maverick's tonight, so I thought this would be fun for them."

"That's nice of you." Emmalyn was one of the kindest women she'd ever met.

"Are you coming tonight?" Emmalyn asked.

"Definitely," she said. "I could use some girl time."

"Isn't it always girls' time?" Hunter drawled. "You two were out here with Kaia last night until almost eleven."

"Did you miss me?" Emmalyn asked Hunter with a sexy smile.

"I always miss you," he said with a laugh. "You know that."

As they exchanged a warm look of love, Lexie cleared her throat. "I need a favor, Hunter."

He gave her a wary look, but there was a softness to his gaze that had grown in the months since he'd met Emmalyn, since he'd left the military and joined a local search and rescue team. He wasn't nearly as intimidating as he'd once been.

"What do you need?" he asked.

"I'd love for you to bring Grayson down to the bar tonight."

"Isn't it women only?"

"Just for the first hour or so while we catch up, but you guys always show up later, so let's just admit that was going to happen."

"I barely know the guy," Hunter protested. "I've said like two sentences to him."

"Exactly. He needs to get to know you. Liam is working a shift tonight while Tyler is out of town. So, Liam and Brad will be at the bar whenever you come, and Madison and Gabe are supposed to show up around eight thirty after they get through dinner service. Let's show Grayson how fun we are in a neutral non-Ocean Shores location."

"I don't see the point," Hunter said.

"The better Grayson knows us, the more personally invested he'll be in our lives, and how they'll change if he sells the building. It's like naming the lobster in the tank before you cook it. Once you've named it, it's much harder to kill."

"So, we're lobsters now?" Hunter said with a laugh.

"For this scenario, yes. That's exactly what we are."

"Maybe you can use Frank, Hunter," Emmalyn said. "He and Grayson have been working on the car today. Why don't you go out to the parking lot and ask them if they want to have a drink with you tonight."

"Great idea," she said to Emmalyn.

"I think so," Emmalyn agreed, with a smile.

Hunter rolled his eyes. "Fine, I'll talk to them, and you two can watch the kids until Bree and Paige get back."

"Deal," she said as Hunter got up, threw on his T-shirt, and walked out to the parking lot.

"I can watch the kids," Emmalyn said, "if you have other things to do."

"I have some emails to answer, but I can sit for a bit."

"Did you finish developing your photos? I want to see the prints. The digital ones you showed us last night looked amazing. I told Hunter we should check out the caves one day. He said he's game."

That wasn't surprising. Hunter had flown helicopters into war zones. He had a high tolerance for risk. "Just make sure you watch the tides carefully when you go. I thought we had way more time than we did. If Grayson hadn't kept his eyes on his watch, we might have had a more harrowing escape. The water came in very fast."

Emmalyn shivered. "Maybe I don't want to go."

"You just have to be careful and smart about it. I got distracted taking my photos. If I'd just been exploring, I wouldn't have stayed inside nearly as long." She paused. "Did I tell you I found a locket in the cave?"

"No, that's exciting. I wonder how long it was there."

"More than thirty years," she said. "It turns out it belonged to Josie. She lost it a long time ago and had no idea it had fallen off when she was exploring the caves."

"That's amazing," Emmalyn said with wonder in her eyes. "And you brought it back to her. There's something about the symmetry of that..." Her voice trailed off. "It feels a little magical. What else did she say about the locket?"

"Not much. But she had a sad and secretive smile on her face. There's definitely a story there."

"I bet it's a good one."

"Maybe someday Josie will tell us," she said.

"She probably will. Have you talked to Grayson since your adventure to the caves?"

"No. That's why I need Hunter to get him down to the bar, so the rest of you can charm him."

"Do you really think we can change his mind?"

"I don't know," she admitted. "But until the decision is made, I won't stop trying."

"Then I'll make sure Hunter does his part, and if tonight doesn't work out, we'll try something else tomorrow and the next day. I love this place, too. It's where I found myself and the love of my life."

"Both are equally important," she said, her gaze drifting toward the entrance. "Maybe it's a good thing Hunter hasn't come back yet. Hopefully, he's talking to Frank and Grayson."

"I'm sure he is, and he also knows a thing or two about

engines, so I have a feeling he might have jumped in to help," Emmalyn said. "But I'm fine here, so do what you need to, and I'll meet you at six to walk to Maverick's."

"Perfect."

As she returned to her apartment, she really hoped Hunter could convince Grayson to join them at the bar, solely because they needed to keep putting pressure on him, and not because she hadn't talked to him since yesterday morning and couldn't stop thinking about him. At least, that was her story, and she was sticking to it.

By eight that night, Lexie was getting restless. While she was enjoying her time with her friends, there was no sign of Hunter or Grayson, and she was beginning to think they might not show up. Drumming her fingers on the table while Emmalyn was relating a funny story from her kindergarten class, she glanced around the bar, wondering if Grayson would even enjoy Maverick's. It probably wasn't his kind of bar. He was a sophisticated man, and Maverick's was anything but sophisticated.

Old surfboards hung from the wooden-beamed ceiling, and black-and-white photos of legendary surfers covered the walls. The weathered floors had been worn smooth by years of sandy feet and dancing, and the salty sea air mingled with the scent of beer and grilled burgers wafting from the kitchen. Maverick's wasn't fancy, but it had soul—a perfect reflection of their coastal community.

"Hello?" Kaia's sharp voice pierced through her reverie, and she started, realizing that Kaia, Ava, Serena, and Emmalyn were looking at her with curiosity and a little concern. "Where did you go, Lexie?" Kaia asked.

"Sorry. I was just thinking about something else."

"Or someone else?" Kaia asked with a knowing gleam in her eyes.

"He'll be here," Emmalyn said. "Hunter told me he agreed to come."

"Who's he? Who's coming?" Ava asked in confusion.

"Grayson," she replied. "I asked Hunter to bring him down so he could get to know the guys and hang out at the bar with Brad and Liam."

"Are you sure you want him here to talk to the guys?" Kaia asked, her gaze pointed.

She shook her head. "Stop trying to make something out of nothing, Kaia." While she hadn't told anyone about kissing Grayson, they did know he'd gone to the caves with her, and there had been more than a few suggestions and teasing questions about just how far she was willing to go to save the apartment building.

"Okay, I'll stop teasing you," Kaia said. "I know you're doing this for all of us, so we are grateful."

"I offered to go over the report I had you send him months ago," Ava put in. "He was very polite and completely uninterested."

"I don't think numbers will sway him," she said. "But since I've gotten to know him a little, I feel like there's more to him than just the ruthless businessman who is only thinking about the bottom line." She let out a sigh. "Or maybe that's just what I want to think because time is running out."

"We still have a few weeks," Emmalyn said, giving her a sympathetic look. "Do you want me to text Hunter?"

Before she could answer, Hunter and Grayson entered the bar, and she felt both relieved and a little nervous as they made their way across the room. Her chest tightened as Grayson's gaze drifted to hers. *Why did he have to be so damned good-looking?*

Dressed in dark jeans and a blue button-down shirt, he looked more like the man who'd explored the caves with her and less like the businessman in the designer suit that had shown up a week ago.

"Now, you can relax," Emmalyn said. "He's here, and Hunter is getting him a drink at the bar."

She felt anything but relaxed, but she gave Emmalyn a smile. "You're right. Sorry I drifted off in the middle of your story."

"Oh, you didn't miss a thing. I think I've bored you all enough with stories of five-year-olds."

"They're always funny," Kaia said.

"Where's Ben these days?" Serena asked. "I don't feel like I've seen him in a while."

"My brother is at a wedding in Hawaii, the lucky guy. He'll be back tomorrow."

"Be sure to introduce him to Grayson," she urged Kaia. "Grayson needs to know our building is serving the community. You're a paramedic. Ben is a cop. Hunter is involved in search and rescue."

"I will," Kaia promised. "But you need to chill, Lexie. You're not going to solve this problem tonight."

She knew that, but she couldn't help moving her gaze to Grayson and Hunter, who were talking to Brad at the bar. They seemed to be getting along, drinking what looked like whiskey, and sharing conversation.

Grayson really was a handsome man. A yearning knot tightened in her gut as she imagined being in his arms again...

It was still surprising to her that she found Grayson so attractive, so desirable. She'd hated him at their first meeting and been annoyed with him for months when he never replied to her emails. She'd thought she'd have trouble even tolerating his stay at Ocean Shores, but now, she felt much differently.

"Lexie, are you in?" Kaia asked.

She gave her a blank look. "Uh, for what?"

"Another pitcher of margaritas."

"Sure. I'll go to the bar and get us one."

"And get me a nonalcoholic one," Serena put in.

"Okay," she said, happy to make her way to the bar. As she

got up from the table, she purposefully did not look back to see the knowing smile on Kaia's face.

When she got to the bar, she said, "Hi, guys. Brad, we need another pitcher of margaritas, and a virgin one for your wife."

"Got it," Brad said.

She smiled at Hunter, then at Grayson. "It's nice to see you both here."

"Hunter suggested I check it out," Grayson replied. "He said you're having a girls' night."

"We try to get together here a few times a month to catch up. The guys usually give us an hour or so to do that before they show up. How's the Mustang coming along?" she asked. "I heard you and Frank were working on it today."

"It's going well. Hunter helped us with an issue we'd been stuck on, so that really changed things up."

"You and Frank were almost there," Hunter said.

"We were close, but we'd been close for an hour before you showed up," Grayson said. "At any rate, the car is in good shape, and Frank should be able to have it ready for the show next Saturday."

As Brad set down the pitcher of margaritas and a separate drink for Serena, Hunter said, "I'll take this to the table for you, Lexie."

"Okay, thanks." She looked back at Grayson. "Do you want to come and sit with us?"

"I'm going to finish this drink and go. I have an early call tomorrow with an associate in London."

"Of course. I'm glad you made it, though."

"Me, too." He finished his whiskey but didn't immediately move to leave. "So, how did the photographs come out?"

"Amazing," she said, finally feeling more comfortable with the turn in the conversation. "I can't wait to show them to you. I'm getting the digital prints tomorrow. I developed the film in my apartment, so maybe you can stop by and take a look sometime."

"Definitely. I'm very glad it worked out."

"It more than worked out. Seeing those photos made me realize how much I want to do more of the same, not the caves, but that kind of interesting location shoot that's thoughtful and provocative and takes the viewer of the picture somewhere else, someplace that they didn't even know existed."

"Well, I have to say the caves took me somewhere else."

"But you were there. I hope the photos will take people into that cave even if they're not physically there."

"I love the way your face lights up when you talk about photography," he murmured. "You really love it. Did you always? Were you carrying around cameras when you were a little girl?"

"No, but I loved photos, and I liked to steal my mom's phone and snap pictures when she wasn't looking. I didn't really get into it until after high school when I took a summer photography class. Then I was hooked."

"But you didn't go into photography; you became a lawyer."

"Because that had always been the plan," she said. "It was expected, and I didn't feel like I could change it up." She paused. "Have you ever considered walking away from your father's company?"

"No. I probably like the company more than he does at this point. He's starting to put me in charge of more and more areas, so it feels like it's our company, not just his."

She wasn't thrilled with that response because being the company man he was, he no doubt had to make sure the business was profitable, which would make changing his mind about a potentially lucrative deal much more difficult.

Grayson sipped his drink as he studied her. "You didn't like my answer."

"That's not true. Your answer is how you feel. There's no right or wrong."

"There's not," he agreed. "For what it's worth, I think you made the right choice, Lexie. You hated your life, and when you talk about photography, you light up like a Christmas tree. You're where you should be."

"I'm getting to where I should be. I'm still a work in progress. But I feel like I turned a corner yesterday. I'm going to prioritize my real goals more than the ones that are easy to do and pay the bills and don't make me wonder whether I'm an imposter or the real thing."

"You are definitely the real thing."

"You haven't even seen the photos yet."

"I watched when you took them. I know they're great. But I would like to see them tomorrow." He set down his drink. "I should probably get going."

"I'm ready to go, too," she said. "I have to get up early as well. I'm shooting an engagement photo in the light of dawn, at the bride's request."

"Those brides seem to have a lot of requests," he said dryly.

"Tell me about it. Let me just say goodbye to everyone, and I'll walk back with you."

He followed her over to the table where Hunter had slid into her chair. Before he could get up, she waved him back down.

"I'm going to call it a night. I have an early job tomorrow. I'll see you all at home."

"I'll go with you," Serena said. "I feel tired."

While she was disappointed that she wouldn't be walking back alone with Grayson, maybe it was better to have a chaperone to prevent any future lapses in judgment.

Serena waved goodbye to her husband, and the three of them walked out the door.

"It feels good out here," Serena said. "Was it warm in the bar, or was it just me?"

"It was a little warm," she said as they fell into step with her in the middle, Serena on one side and Grayson on the other. "You only have a couple of weeks to go, right?"

"Two," Serena said with a sigh. "Everyone says I should enjoy being pregnant because once the baby is born, I'll be even more exhausted, but I can't wait to see her. I feel so heavy and crampy all the time. And sorry for complaining."

"You're not complaining, and even if you were, it's understandable."

"Are you sure you should be walking home?" Grayson asked. "I can run back to Ocean Shores, grab my car, and come back and pick you up."

"It's only five blocks from here. I can make it, and the doctor said it's good for me to walk. It keeps the blood flowing, and the baby seems to like it when I'm moving. That's usually when she performs her gymnastics, which involves jumping up and down on my bladder," she added with a laugh.

"Sounds awesome," Grayson said dryly.

"It is," Serena said with a twinkle in her eye. "How are you enjoying Ocean Shores? Are you feeling the magic yet?"

"You do have a good group," he admitted.

"It's your group, too. You own the building," Serena pointed out. "And now you're living there, so you're one of us."

"For the time being," he said, his tone almost deliberately neutral.

She hated that he hadn't already seen how great everything was. Grayson was the kind of man who set a goal and stuck to it. She was going to have to keep fighting to change his mind.

They had just crossed the street and gone around the corner when Serena suddenly let out a yelp and stopped walking.

"What's wrong?" she asked with concern as Serena bent over. She put a hand on her shoulder. "Are you okay?"

"I don't think so," Serena replied, gasping. "I've been having fake contractions, but this feels like the real thing."

"There are fake contractions?" Grayson asked in bemusement.

Serena nodded, her lips tightening. "Oh, God!"

She looked at Grayson, then at Serena. "Should we go back to the bar?"

"I don't think I can keep walking," Serena said.

"There's a bench over there," Grayson said, helping her walk Serena to the bench. "I'm going to run to Ocean Shores, get my car, and I'll be back as fast as I can. You call Brad. Whoever gets here first can take her to the hospital."

She appreciated his decisiveness and the speed with which he took off. She took out her phone and called Brad, but it went to voicemail. "He's not answering."

"He's probably not near his phone," Serena said. "Maybe it's nothing. It seems to be gone."

"Okay, good, but we still need to get you home or to the hospital."

Serena let out another cry. "Not gone after all," she gasped. "It's really bad, Lexie. What are we going to do?"

CHAPTER TEN

"We're going to hang tight until Grayson gets back, and you're going to try to breathe through the contraction," she said, not really sure what advice she should be giving her. "Take my hand."

Serena's fingers wrapped around hers as she tried to breathe but was clearly in a lot of pain. "I—I think I'm having the baby."

"What? Now?" she asked in shock.

"It feels like something shifted, like the baby is lower." Serena put a hand on her abdomen. "There's a lot of pressure..."

She called Brad again, but he didn't answer. She was about to start hitting up the rest of her friends at the bar when Grayson pulled up on the street in front of them with squealing brakes. Before they could move, another contraction doubled Serena over.

"It's going to be okay," she reassured her. "Grayson and I will take you to the hospital. I'll get a hold of Brad, and he'll meet us there."

"I'm scared, Lexie."

"I know. But you can do this, Serena. You're a very strong person."

Serena blew out a breath, her face red, sweat dotting her skin. "I think the worst is over for now."

With Grayson's help, she got Serena into the back seat of his car and climbed in next to her. "Drive to the hospital," she told Grayson, giving him the name of the nearest medical center. "I'll keep calling Brad."

"I could stop at the bar—"

His suggestion was cut off by another piercing scream from Serena.

"Never mind. Hospital," Grayson said, turning on his GPS.

When Serena's contraction eased, she punched in Brad's number again, relieved beyond belief when he picked up.

"Hey, Lexie. Did you forget something?" he asked.

"No. I'm with Serena. She went into labor on the way home."

"What?" he shouted. "That's not possible. Where are you?"

"Grayson is driving us to the hospital. I've been calling you for several minutes."

"I just went back into the kitchen to talk to our chef. How is she doing?"

"I'm scared," Serena cried. "You better hurry, Brad. This baby is coming fast."

"I'll meet you at the hospital," he promised. "Hang in there, honey."

"I'm trying, but it really hurts." As another contraction hit, Serena squeezed her hand and yelled again, swearing like Lexie had never heard her swear before.

Brad had already ended the call, so she put her phone into her pocket and focused on Serena. "Try to breathe in and out," she said soothingly. "We're going to be at the hospital in like two minutes. You can do this, Serena."

"I'm not sure I have two minutes, Lex. I can feel the baby."

She could see the terror in her eyes. "Try not to push," she said, not sure if that was the right advice or not, but she really didn't want Serena to have her baby in the back of Grayson's car.

Thankfully, Grayson was driving fast, and a minute later, they pulled up in front of the ER. Grayson jumped out and ran into the building to get help.

She opened her car door. "Can you get out, Serena?"

"I can try," Serena said, sliding toward the door. As she swung her feet to the ground, Grayson returned with a nurse and a wheelchair. They helped Serena out of the car and into the chair and then rushed her inside as Serena began to cry again.

"I'll park the car and meet you in there," Grayson said.

"Okay, thanks." She blew out a breath as she made her way into the ER. The woman at the information desk told her that Serena was already on her way up to maternity, which was on the third floor. She could join her there.

She went back outside and waited for Grayson, who came running up to the door with Brad at his side.

"How is she?" Brad asked, his face worried and stressed.

"They've taken her up to maternity. It's on the third floor."

"Tell me how she's doing, Lexie," he begged as they raced inside. "It sounded like she was in a lot of pain."

"The contractions were fast and rough," she said as they moved down the hall and into the elevator. "We were just walking back from the bar, and she suddenly had a horrible pain. It kept coming back, every couple of minutes. I called you as soon as it happened."

"I know. I can't believe I didn't have my phone. I've been keeping it close to me, but I didn't think anything was going to happen so soon."

She could see the guilt in his eyes. "You couldn't have known, Brad. She's not due for two more weeks. And it all came on so fast. You're here now. That's what matters."

"I hope she's all right and I'm not too late." Brad jumped off the elevator as soon as the doors opened.

She and Grayson followed more slowly, watching as Brad was waved through a set of double doors.

"I hope he gets to her before she has the baby," she murmured to Grayson.

"I wouldn't bet on it. I thought she was going to have the baby in my car."

She met his gaze. "I was afraid that was going to happen, too."

He ran a hand through his hair as he let out a breath. "That was intense. But you did good." Admiration filled his eyes. "You kept her calm."

"I tried, but I was having a hard time not panicking myself." She moved across the waiting room, sat down on a couch, and let out a breath. "I thought childbirth was supposed to go really slow in the beginning. I'm so glad you were with us, Grayson. I don't know what I would have done. I probably would have had to call 911 from the bench on the sidewalk."

"I'm glad I was there, too," he said.

"I hope there's nothing wrong. The labor came on so suddenly. I don't think I can fully relax until she has the baby, and I know both of them are healthy and safe."

"I guess that means you want to stay here," he said with a knowing gleam in his eyes.

"I do. But you don't have to stay, Grayson. I know you have to get up early tomorrow. I can get a rideshare home."

"Don't you have a photo shoot at dawn?"

She shrugged. "This is more important. I'll manage on whatever sleep I get. The way things were going, I think the baby will be here soon."

"I agree. I'll wait with you for a while."

They sat in silence, the adrenaline of the last twenty minutes slowly wearing off. Around them, the waiting room hummed with quiet activity—nurses at the desk, some going in and out of the double doors, others speaking with anxious visitors.

As she looked at the clock on the wall, Grayson gave her a smile. "It hasn't been that long."

"I know. I'm just nervous and impatient."

"Serena is a healthy young woman, and there's no reason to think she won't be okay."

"Except what we just witnessed."

"Well, I don't know anything about women in labor, so I'm

no expert, but it seems to me like there's usually a lot of pain and yelling involved," he said dryly.

"And swearing. I've never heard Serena swear like that."

He laughed. "I was surprised, too. But I wasn't sure if she was always like that."

"Never. Absolutely never." She paused. "I do appreciate you staying with me."

"If I went home, I'd just be wondering what was going on."

He'd no sooner finished speaking when the double doors opened, and Brad walked out. She jumped to her feet, but she didn't even have to ask Brad if Serena was okay, because he was smiling from ear to ear, a joyous glow in his eyes. "Serena is fine and the baby is beautiful. She's seven pounds, eight ounces, and when she opened her eyes, she screamed her head off, which reminded me very much of her mother right before she was born."

"Oh, Brad, I'm so happy for you." She gave him a hug.

"Congratulations," Grayson said, shaking Brad's hand.

"I have to get back to her. Can you let everyone know, Lexie?"

"I will spread the word. Tell Serena I'm glad she's okay. And I can't wait to see the baby."

As he headed back to his wife, she turned to Grayson. "It's all good. Just like you said."

"Told you," he returned with a smug smile.

She knew she shouldn't, but she couldn't stop herself from hugging him and brushing a grateful kiss against his lips. "Thank you."

"I didn't do anything."

She gazed into his eyes. "Yes, you did. You got Serena here, and you stayed. And I'm just really happy they're okay."

As they broke apart, she heard familiar voices and turned around to see her friends coming into the waiting room. Everyone from the bar was there: Kaia, Ava, Liam, Emmalyn, and Hunter.

"Serena had the baby," she told them. "Everyone is healthy. Brad is over the moon. It's all good."

"Thank God," Ava said, practically collapsing in Liam's arms. "I was so worried about her. She saw the doctor yesterday, and he didn't think she was going to be early."

"It all worked out," Liam said. "I told you."

"I know. I was just scared for her." Ava turned to her. "Thank you for getting her here, Lexie."

"That was Grayson. I just held her hand and tried to pretend I knew what she was supposed to do. I really wished you'd walked home with us," she added to Kaia. "I was afraid she was going to have the baby in the car."

"That would have been messy," Kaia said. "But I'm sure you did great."

"She did," Grayson confirmed.

"We should go home," Hunter said. "Aside from Ava and Liam, they'd probably rather keep the visiting circle small tonight."

She nodded in agreement. "I think so, too."

"We'll stay," Ava confirmed.

"Do you want a ride, Lexie?" Kaia asked.

"Actually, I left my bag in Grayson's car, so I'll just ride with him."

"Sounds good," Kaia said.

"I can't believe she had the baby," Emmalyn murmured as they rode down to the lobby. "She's going to be the youngest tenant at Ocean Shores."

Emmalyn's words rang through her head as she walked with Grayson to his car, and she couldn't help wondering how long Serena's baby would even be able to live at Ocean Shores. All their previous plans of helping Serena and Brad with babysitting might turn into an impossibility if they were all scattered to different buildings around the city.

Grayson drove them home without a word. She didn't know if he was thinking the same thing she was or if he was just tired.

But either way, she wasn't going to get into a fight with him tonight, not after everything he'd done. And all that mattered now was that Serena and her baby were healthy. Whatever other problems there were could be dealt with tomorrow.

———

After Grayson got off his London call on Monday morning, he punched in his father's number. It was eight o'clock in the morning, but his dad had always been an early riser.

"Grayson," his father said. "How are you? Did you speak to Morgan in London this morning?"

"I just did."

"And..."

"The deal is moving along, but that's not why I'm calling."

"Okay. Why are you calling?"

"You need to let me out of this deal at Ocean Shores. I can't stay here any longer."

"Why not?"

"Because this is crazy." He ran his hand through his hair in frustration. "I can't make business decisions about this place while I'm living here. I can't pretend to be their friend when I'm on the verge of evicting everyone. It makes no sense."

"It's a couple of weeks, Grayson."

"Why do you want me here? What is it you want me to learn?"

"When you know the answer to that question, then it will be time for you to leave. Until then, I'd like you to honor our agreement. It's not that much to ask. And you can work from there. I don't see the problem."

"You don't see it because you're not here. You're not getting invited to barbecues and drinks and rushing a pregnant woman to the hospital only to think about how she and her husband might be losing their apartment in a few months."

"You rushed a pregnant woman to the hospital?"

"Yes, and you're missing the point."

"I got the point. You're getting caught up in the community, and you don't like it."

"Exactly. No matter how much I care about these people, it doesn't change the fact that this building is more valuable if we sell it."

"I understand that's your position. You know mine. We'll talk in a few weeks. Or you can leave now, and I'll take back the management and oversight of the building."

"If you don't want to sell it, Dad, why don't you just say that?" he asked with annoyance.

"It's not that simple. I have a meeting, Grayson. I'll talk to you later."

His father was gone before he could utter another word. He tossed the phone down in disgust. He didn't understand what it was he was supposed to get out of this entire experience. But his father had always been good at getting what he wanted and now was no exception. If he was going to get what he wanted, then he had to stick it out. He just needed to stop getting so involved with everyone, especially Lexie. She was starting to take up more and more of his time. Even when he wasn't with her, he was thinking about her, and last night's shared experience had only bonded them more.

He leaned back in his chair, staring at his computer screen without seeing it, when he heard someone outside. No one knocked or rang the bell. Instead, a large envelope was slipped under his door. He got up and walked over to pick it up.

Opening the flap, he pulled out a photo with a sticky note attached. "*A small preview. Can't wait to show you more, Lexie.*"

The photograph was one she'd taken of him standing in the entrance to the cave, the filtered light creating a magical, mystical feeling, and the expression on his face was one of wonder and bemusement, which described exactly how he'd felt that day.

He stared at the picture for a long, long time, because it

wasn't just how detailed, how absolutely perfect the composition was; it was because he barely recognized himself. The man in this photo felt more like an adventurer than a businessman, more like someone who was a part of nature, not a part of buying and selling buildings. This guy looked like he'd suddenly discovered another side of himself.

He didn't want to see that side. He put the picture back in the envelope. But even tucked away, the image lingered—and he knew that was exactly why Lexie had given it to him.

CHAPTER ELEVEN

Somehow, Grayson managed to avoid Lexie for four days. They'd exchanged a few texts with her inviting him to see the rest of the photographs, but he'd told her he had a busy week and would have to catch up with her on the weekend.

He'd spent most of the week at a local workspace, where it was easier to concentrate on business. Then he'd grab dinner out and head home around nine. Usually by then, the courtyard was empty, so there was less of a chance he would run into people. That was his new plan—stay at Ocean Shores but keep his distance.

After parking his car in the lot, he walked into the courtyard and ran into Brad, who was holding his beautiful baby daughter in his arms. "You're home," he said.

Brad gave him a beaming smile. "We are. This is Amanda Jane Morrison." He pulled the blanket away from her face to give Grayson a better look.

"She's beautiful," he said, amazed by the beauty of her perfect, tiny features and her dark hair. "How's Serena feeling?"

"Tired but good. She wanted to go to bed early tonight, and this little princess was not cooperating, so I thought I'd bring her outside. She quieted down as soon as the fresh air hit her face."

"She's looking all around," he commented, noting the baby's wide-eyed look of wonder. "Taking everything in."

"She does that a lot, especially at night. The doctor said her days and nights are mixed up. I'll be happy when that changes," he said, stifling a yawn. As the baby started to fuss, he said, "I better keep walking. She likes to move."

"Have a good night." He was about to head up the stairs when he heard a loud banging noise coming from the direction of Lexie's apartment. He walked around the pool, realizing the clanging sound was actually coming from the apartment next door, which belonged to Kaia. Her curtains were partly drawn, with only a dim light glowing inside.

He put his hands on the window as he looked into the room, wondering where the banging noise was coming from. It didn't appear that Kaia was home, and Lexie's apartment looked dark, too. He needed to get Josie to open the door so they could see what was happening.

As he started to turn around, a man grabbed his arms and shoved him up against the window frame.

"What the hell?" he swore, struggling to get away, but the man was strong and determined.

"Who are you?" the man demanded in a sharp voice. "What are you doing peering through my sister's window?"

Grayson tried to turn around, but the man's grip tightened. "I heard a noise—"

"I asked who you are." The man spun him around, and Grayson found himself face-to-face with a tall, broad-shouldered guy who had cop written all over him, even in jeans and a T-shirt.

"Grayson Holt. I live here. And I was looking in Kaia's window because I heard a banging noise."

"Ben! What are you doing?" Kaia yelled as she jogged down the hall in her paramedic uniform, keys jangling in her hand. And right behind her was Lexie.

"I caught this guy looking in your window," Ben said.

"Because something is going on in your apartment, Kaia," Grayson interjected. "If you would all just listen for one second."

As they fell silent, the banging from inside became very clear.

"Oh, my God! What is that?" Kaia asked. "Is someone in there?"

Ben grabbed Kaia's keys and opened the door. As Ben stepped inside, he switched on the lights, and Kaia followed. Because Grayson wanted to know what was going on, he moved into the apartment, and so did Lexie.

The noise was coming from the far corner of the living room. An oscillating fan had been left running, but it had tilted just enough that every sweep sent it smacking into the side of a bookcase. The impact made the whole shelf tremble, rattling the framed photos on top until one toppled over with a clatter.

Kaia let out a disbelieving laugh and strode across the room to turn off the fan. "I was in a rush this morning. I guess I left it on, and it fell over. Sorry about all this. Ben, you owe Grayson an apology."

Ben didn't look convinced. "He was looking in your window, and you told me some guy has had a hard time taking no for an answer."

"That's all resolved now," Kaia said.

"Grayson is the owner of Ocean Shores, Ben," Lexie interjected. "He's staying here for a month."

"Oh, right," Ben said, realization suddenly running through his gaze. "I thought your name sounded familiar. I'm sorry." He awkwardly cleared his throat. "I hope I didn't hurt you."

"I'll live," he said shortly.

"Kaia is my sister, and when I saw you looking in her window..."

"I understand. You were protecting your sister."

"You have a bruise on your face," Lexie said, her gaze narrowing with concern. Then she shot Ben a dark look. "Did you hit him?"

"I just shoved him."

"I'm fine," he said quickly. "It was a misunderstanding. And now, I'll say goodnight."

As he walked out of the apartment, Lexie followed him to the stairs. "Are you sure you're okay, Grayson?"

"I told you I was."

"I just want you to know that Ben is a good guy. He's a cop, and he has quick reactions when he thinks there's trouble. Usually, it's a good thing. He actually saved Emmalyn from a bad situation several months ago."

"Don't worry about it, Lexie."

She stared back at him, uncertainty in her gaze. And even in the evening light, with her hair pulled back in a messy ponytail and concern creasing her brow, she was beautiful in a way that stole his breath. He knew he should go upstairs and into his apartment, but now that she was standing right in front of him, it was difficult to walk away. "Were you out tonight?" he asked.

"Yes. I took photos at a woman's ninetieth birthday party. It was actually fun. She's a live wire, and she loves to line dance, so everyone had to get up and join in. I think some of the younger ones got tired before she did. It was nice to see someone really living every minute of their life."

"She sounds like a spirited woman."

"She is. Also very opinionated, but I enjoyed talking to her. She told me the secret to not just a long life but also a happy life is to never make decisions in fear or anger and to look at change as an opportunity, not a setback."

"That sounds like good advice."

"I thought so, too." She paused. "I still want to show you the photos I took in the cave."

"It's late."

"Not tonight—maybe tomorrow. What are your plans this weekend?"

"I'm not sure. I may drive out to Palm Springs to see some property I'm interested in purchasing."

Her gaze suddenly lit up. "Palm Springs? That's really close to Joshua Tree. I've been thinking about getting out there to take some photos. The trees are amazingly twisted creations that look like aliens. There are also rock formations and a cactus garden. I have a photo on my dining room wall that I'd like to replace with one of my own." She paused. "I guess you know where this is going..."

"You want to come along," he said, not at all sure how he felt about that.

"It would be more fun to go with someone. And if you haven't seen the park, you might enjoy it. You loved the caves. This could be another great trip."

That's what he was afraid of. Because more great experiences with her weren't part of his game plan to maintain distance and make an objective decision about the building. But seeing the light of excitement in her eyes along with a hopeful plea, he could not even consider saying no.

"It does sound interesting," he said.

"Is that a yes?"

"Yes."

"Great. I'm excited. I'm going to do more research so that I know exactly where we should go and what we should look for."

"We'll talk about it tomorrow."

"Okay. Goodnight, Grayson."

"Goodnight," he murmured as he finally did what he should have done a few minutes earlier: go up the stairs and into his apartment. But he couldn't be that unhappy about setting up another adventurous outing with Lexie. He'd missed talking to her the past few days. And maybe he needed to stop working so hard to stay away from her and just enjoy the time they had before he left, because it was all going to end in a little over two weeks.

Lexie was still excited about her upcoming trip to Joshua Tree when she woke up Friday morning. She told herself it was just about the photographs, but she knew it was also about Grayson. She'd missed talking to him the past few days, and while she was sorry Ben had roughed him up the night before, she was glad that the incident had brought them back together.

But before Sunday, she had work to do, and she needed to concentrate on that. While most of her time was spent on her photography business, she also helped her aunt with random issues around the building. To that end, she opened the billing portal and realized their newest tenant had not yet paid his rent. He still had a day to go, but she was concerned. So, she headed over to her aunt's apartment a little after nine.

"It smells like a bakery in here," she said as Josie opened her door.

"That's because I've been baking," Josie said, her cheeks flushed, a streak of flour across her forehead.

She followed her aunt into the kitchen as a timer went off. While her aunt liked to bake, she was surprised to see her pull a batch of cookies from the oven while there were already two pans of brownies cooling on the counter. "Are you participating in a bake sale?"

"No, but I have friends who need sweets."

"Like..."

"Serena and Brad. They love my oatmeal raisin cookies, and with the new baby, they could use a little sugar for those late-night feeds."

"That's a good idea."

"And my friend Joan is going through chemotherapy, so I'm going to drop her off some brownies this afternoon. What brings you by? I heard about what happened last night outside of Kaia's apartment. I ran into Ben this morning, and he apologized for shoving Grayson into the wall when he thought he was a stalker."

"That was not good," she said. "I came in from the parking

lot with Kaia, and we heard shouting. I couldn't believe it when I saw Ben had Grayson pinned against the wall. Every time I think we're convincing Grayson how great we are, something happens to change that picture."

Her aunt gave her a small smile. "Life has a way of surprising us. Ben said Grayson wasn't hurt. But was he angry?"

"He said it was no big deal. But that seems to be his go-to phrase."

"Well, I hope it wasn't a big deal. Is that why you came by?"

"No. I was checking the rents, and I noticed our new tenant still hasn't paid."

"It's not the fifteenth yet," her aunt said with a dismissive wave, as she started moving the cookies from the pan onto a cooling rack.

"Well, it's not a good sign that he's waiting until the last day."

"It's not a sign at all. If he doesn't pay by tomorrow, then we can talk about it."

"No one has seen him around. What's his deal?"

"He's a busy person and also very private. But I'm sure he'll slowly integrate into our community. You just have to give him time. Look at Hunter now. He was once the mystery man everyone was wondering about."

"Yes, but we all knew he'd been injured on duty, and he was healing. We don't know anything about Jax Ridley."

"I know you're curious, Lexie. But I promised him privacy, and I'm going to stick to that."

She frowned at her aunt's words. "I'm not just anybody. I can keep a secret, you know."

"I'm aware of that. It's not personal. It's just a promise I made." Her aunt smiled. "How about some brownies? I know you love them."

She was about to say no when she wondered if she could get in on her aunt's baking and make her own gift offering. "I'm good, but maybe I could take some to Grayson, as an apology for what happened last night."

Her aunt's eyes sparkled. "That sounds like a great idea. And it will give you another chance to talk to him." She paused. "But these need to cool before I take them out of the pan. Why don't you come back in an hour or so and pick them up? I'll put the ones for Grayson on the white plate. And the ones for Joan on the blue plate. I'm heading out shortly to get my hair colored, which, as you know, is a long process, so just let yourself in."

"Okay," she said, distracted by the incoming text on her phone. "Oh, man, more problems," she muttered.

"What's wrong?"

"I'm shooting a family portrait this morning, and the baby woke up early, so they want to move up the shoot before the next naptime. I better run."

"I'll see you later."

After leaving Josie, she made a brief stop at her apartment to pack up her equipment and then headed out the door.

She met the Holmquist family in a park by their home and spent the next hour trying to get the perfect shot of the young family, which consisted of Ray and Gretchen Holmquist, and their three kids: a five-year-old boy, a three-year-old girl, and a seven-month-old baby girl, who didn't like the headband on her head, wanted to crawl instead of stay in her mother's arms, and was generally unhappy for most of the time.

With patience and care, she managed to capture a dozen or so shots that they loved, but it was almost noon when she was done, and she ran home to get a quick bite before her afternoon engagement photo shoot at a nearby cove.

She ate a quick lunch while answering emails and then got ready to go again. As she was about to leave, she remembered the brownies and decided to stop by her aunt's apartment and get them since Grayson's car was in the lot and he was probably home.

Her aunt was still at her hair appointment, so she let herself in and walked into the kitchen. As she was about to grab one of the plates of brownies, she couldn't help noticing a check on the counter from their mysterious tenant. His name was on the check, and the address was Ocean Shores, so it looked like he'd already had new checks made, but that gave her no further clue as to where he was from before he'd moved in. Well, her aunt would get to keep her secrets a while longer, and so would this Jax Ridley. At least he'd paid his rent. That was one less thing to worry about. She grabbed the plate of brownies and headed out the door.

As she neared Grayson's apartment, a little shiver of anticipation ran down her spine. It was amazing how she'd gone from dreading his entire visit to feeling excited at the prospect of seeing him. She really needed to find a way to tamp that excitement down because it had nowhere to actually go. But she couldn't worry about that now.

As the knock came at his door, Grayson's body tightened. He knew it was Lexie. Maybe it was her knock, or maybe it was just that she was the most likely person to show up at his apartment, but he couldn't stop the burst of energy that sent him to the door, eager to see her pretty face.

"Hi," she said, giving him a tentative smile that just about undid him. "You look good. Are you on your way out?"

"Just got back from an early morning meeting in Newport Beach."

"That explains the suit. You look very Wall Street right now."

"What's up?"

She held out the plate in her hand. "Peace offering. For Ben's actions last night. I know you said it was no big deal, but I'm sure it was disturbing to have some stranger shove you up against a wall."

"It was a first," he admitted. "But it seems like Ben should be making this offer, not you."

"Ben can't cook. Trust me. He took over the grill at one of our parties, and it was a disaster. We had to order pizza."

He smiled. "There's really no need for this, Lexie."

"There's never a need for brownies, but they're still delicious. To be completely honest, I didn't make them; Josie did."

"So, Josie made you brownies to give to me on Ben's behalf? Do I have that right?" he teased.

"Well, it wasn't exactly like that," she said, smiling back at him. "Just enjoy. Don't overthink it."

"Okay. Do you want one?"

"I have to run to another shoot, so maybe later. Are you working here today?"

"I am."

"Maybe I'll see you later then."

"Maybe," he said as he shut the door.

For the next few hours, he focused on work because if he didn't, he wouldn't stop thinking about Lexie and how much he wanted to kiss her again. She'd suggested meeting up later, but that was a bad idea, and he should probably make sure that didn't happen.

Tired of working and dealing with the conflict going on in his head, he got up from the table and moved into the kitchen, his gaze catching on the plate of brownies Lexie had dropped by earlier. He unwrapped the cellophane, the whiff of chocolate making his stomach rumble. He grabbed one, then another. They tasted absolutely delicious.

He took one more brownie and sat back down in front of his computer, reading his assistant's latest email. More problems in Singapore. He told her they'd talk in the morning. She reacted with surprise a few seconds later, asking if he was sick. He smiled to himself, telling her he was fine, but he needed a break, and she should take one, too.

As he closed his email program, he had to admit the brownies had made him feel remarkably better about the day. In fact, he wanted to go outside and get some air, feel the sun on his face.

Grabbing his keys, he headed out the door. He met up with Emmalyn at the bottom of the stairs.

"Hello," he said cheerfully. "How are you today?"

She looked a little surprised. "I'm good. How about you?"

"Couldn't be better."

"Where are you off to?" she asked.

"The sand and the sea are calling my name," he said.

"Oh, okay. Enjoy yourself."

He moved through the parking lot as the white sand and sparkling blue-green sea beckoned to him.

CHAPTER TWELVE

When Lexie entered the courtyard shortly after five, there were several people around the pool, which wasn't surprising since it was a warm Friday afternoon.

Josie was at the nearest table, and when she saw her, she jumped to her feet. "Lexie," she said sharply. "I've called you several times."

"Is something wrong?" she asked, moving over to the table where Josie had been playing cards with Margaret, Frank, and Emmalyn.

"Did you take the blue plate of brownies?"

"Uh...I took a plate. Why?"

"Where are they now? Are they in your apartment?"

"No. I gave them to Grayson hours ago. I told you I was going to."

"Oh no. You have to get them back," Josie said, unusual worry in her eyes. "You took the wrong plate of brownies, Lexie. You took the ones I made for Joan. And they were...enhanced."

"Enhanced?" she echoed. "What do you mean?"

"They had a special ingredient to help with her chemo symptoms."

"Are you saying..."

Josie met her gaze. "Yes, that's exactly what I'm saying."

"Maybe Grayson didn't eat any. I'll talk to him."

"Grayson left about a half hour ago," Emmalyn interjected. "And what are you guys talking about? What was in the brownies?"

"Weed," she told Emmalyn.

"Oh, wow," Emmalyn said. "That explains it."

"Explains what?"

"I ran into Grayson on his way out, and he was really friendly. He gave me a big smile, and when I asked him where he was going, he said the sand and the sea were calling him."

"Oh, my God! I have to find him. I can't believe I got Grayson high."

"Well, technically, it was me," Josie said. "But I told you to take the white plate."

She ignored her aunt as she ran into the parking lot. Grayson's car was still parked in the lot, so at least he wasn't driving. She jogged out of the lot and across the beach path, pulling off her sandals as she hit the sand. There were at least a couple dozen people on the beach. But Grayson wasn't one of them. She started walking along the sand toward town. Relief washed over her when she spotted him sitting on the sand. His suit coat and tie were tossed over the shoes and socks next to him, and he appeared to be talking to a seagull.

"I know what you're thinking," he said to the bird, which had landed a few feet away from him. "You're thinking, 'What's this guy doing in a suit on my beach?' And that's a fair question. Really fair."

The seagull squawked and took off.

"That was rude," Grayson called after it.

Lexie approached slowly, like she might approach a wild animal. "Grayson?"

He turned toward her with a smile that was brighter and more relaxed than any expression she'd ever seen on his face, just as Emmalyn had described.

"Lexie! Perfect timing. I was just having a philosophical discussion with a seagull about appropriate beach attire."

"I heard."

"Did you know seagulls can live up to fifteen years?"

"I did not. Grayson," she said gently, "how are you feeling?"

"Incredible," he said, spreading his arms wide. "Absolutely fantastic. I can't remember the last time I felt this... relaxed. It's like someone turned down the volume on the noise in my head."

"Did you eat the brownies I brought you?"

"Yes, and they were great. The best brownies I've ever had. Just like this day is the best day I've ever had. Especially now that you're here."

"Really?"

"You're so beautiful, Lexie. How are you still single?"

"Sometimes it's a mystery to me. I need to tell you something."

"Can it wait?" he asked, holding up a seashell. "You need to look at this shell—at the patterns, the lines, the colors. It's like nature's own artwork." He held it out to her, and she could see genuine wonder in his eyes. This wasn't the calculating businessman she'd been sparring with for weeks. This was someone completely unguarded, seeing beauty in a simple seashell.

The shell didn't appear that extraordinary to her—but then, she hadn't had any brownies. "It's pretty." She sat down next to him, having a feeling it would take a little time to explain to Grayson what was going on.

"Think of how many shells get washed up every day, and most people never stop to look at them. They just walk on by. That's what I would normally do." His gaze swung to her. "But you wouldn't walk by. You'd stop. You'd take a picture. You'd make sure everyone in the world could see the beauty of that one shell. Because that's what you do. You should take a picture now. Where's your camera?"

"I left it at home." She realized she'd left everything with her aunt, including her phone, but she wasn't going to worry about that now. They were only a few blocks away from Ocean Shores, and she'd fulfilled her responsibilities for the day.

"Too bad. You should take the shell home or go get your camera."

"I'll come back later with my camera," she promised.

"It might not be here then. You might not ever find it again." His gaze grew serious. "Sometimes you don't appreciate what you have. You let it go. You think there will be time to come back later, but maybe there won't be time. Maybe when it's gone, it's gone, and you never get it back."

It felt like he was talking about something personal, something real, and she found herself liking this open, wondering, philosophical version of Grayson. But this wasn't the real him; this was a drugged version, and it was her fault. As soon as she told him the truth, he'd probably be furious. And all this happiness would end.

"I want to walk," he said, jumping to his feet. He grabbed his tie and tucked it into the coat pocket before throwing his coat over one shoulder. Then he picked up his shoes and held out his free hand. "Walk with me, Lexie."

How could she resist? She stood up and put one hand in his, holding her sandals in the other hand.

They walked down the endless beach, Grayson rambling on with amazement at so many sights she didn't think he would have ever noticed on a normal day, and all the while his fingers clung to hers.

Suddenly, he stopped abruptly, pointing to a weathered shack with picnic tables on the edge of the sand near a sign for Chuck's Chili. "What's this place?"

"They serve hot dogs, burgers, and fries—all with chili," she said with a laugh.

"Is it good?"

"I like it, but it's not fancy."

"I don't want fancy. I want a chili burger and some chili

fries," he said with enthusiasm, his blue eyes lighting up. "Let's go."

"I don't have my wallet."

"I've got mine," he said, patting his pants pocket. "It's on me."

"Are you sure you don't want to go to a nicer place?"

"You said it's good. You're not lying, are you?"

"No. It's good if you like chili."

"And I do." He pulled her across the sand to the restaurant.

They ordered at the counter, then filled their cups with sodas from the fountain and walked outside, grabbing an empty table that was aglow with the setting sun.

"Look at that sky," Grayson said. "All those colors. You should take a picture. Wait, you don't have your phone. Here, take mine."

She waved off the offer of his phone. "It's okay. I've taken a million photos of the sunset over this beach. I need to start getting to other beaches and taking other sunsets."

"We're going to Joshua Tree on Sunday. We should make sure we stay until sunset."

"That would be a good idea," she said, a little chill running down her arms as a gust blew in off the ocean.

His gaze narrowed. "Are you cold? Here, put this on." He pulled his coat off his shoulders to give it to her.

"I'm fine."

"You're not fine. You just shivered." He got up from the table and came around behind her, helping her put on his coat.

She had to admit she felt toasty warm now, not just from the coat, but from the scent of Grayson's cologne that clung to the fabric. "Thanks."

"That's better," he said, sitting down across from her. "You're so pretty, Lexie."

She flushed, knowing it was one thing to let him talk about sunsets and seashells and another to let him talk about her.

"You make it hard to stay away from you," he added.

"Why do you want to stay away from me?"

He met her gaze. "Because I'll be leaving in two weeks. It's not enough time."

"Enough time for what?" She really needed to stop asking questions, but she couldn't seem to stop. Grayson was normally so guarded. She had to take the opportunity in front of her.

"You know what," he replied.

Her cheeks grew warm at the look in his eyes. "I—I don't know what to say."

"There's nothing to say or do. It is what it is." He looked more somber now. "I just wish we'd met somewhere else, under different circumstances."

"If that were the case, you probably wouldn't have looked at me twice."

"Not true. Once I saw you, I wouldn't have been able to stop looking at you."

"We live in different worlds, Grayson."

"I want to live in your world. I want to have adventures. I have never felt as alive as I did when we went into that cave together. I thought I was a risk-taker, but that was only in business, not in life. I took a risk that day. So did you."

She nodded. "I needed to push myself. But I might have chickened out if you hadn't been with me."

"You're brave. You would have done it."

"I don't know about that. But I'm glad you were with me, and I want to have more experiences like that, too." She paused. "There's nothing stopping you from doing the same. Just because you run a company doesn't mean you can't have adventures."

"My father didn't. He worked nonstop his whole life. He was always the first man in to work and the last man out, and that's what he taught me to do. He said that's how you make it. And I can't argue with his success."

"But do you think he sacrificed other parts of his life to be at work?"

"I know he did. You can put my mother at the top of that list. They've been living separately for years."

"That's sad."

"Actually, I think they're both fine with it."

"Are you also on the list?"

"Right behind my mother. I know my father loves me, but growing up, he was never around, and when he was, he was working. He didn't keep his friends, either. He didn't make time for them, not the way you do." He paused. "I don't think I make time for my friends, either. I need to do better, Lexie."

"You will," she said with encouragement. "Relationships take time and effort, but it's always worth it."

"But how do you know if someone is genuine or if they're just using you to get ahead, to get something?"

"Uh, I'm not sure. I haven't had that problem. I don't have anything anyone wants. But I'm sure you have friends who genuinely care about you."

"Maybe a few, but, like I said, I haven't made time for friends. My grandmother once told me I shouldn't always follow my father's example, that I should aim higher. He missed the last Christmas we could have spent together before she passed away. Not that he knew it would be her last, but it was."

She thought about his words, wondering why a workaholic like his father would have sent Grayson to Ocean Shores. "Why do you think he wanted you to live in the building for a month?"

"Hell if I know," he muttered. "I've asked him, and he just says I won't have to ask when I figure out the answer, whatever that means." He jumped to his feet when their number was called. "Time for chili." He hurried into the shack to pick up their food, returning a moment later with a burger, hot dog, and fries, all topped with Chuck's chili as well as onions and cheese. He cut the burger and the dog in half, so that they could each try both dishes, and then they shared the fries.

It was probably the unhealthiest meal she'd had in weeks, but it was also absolutely delicious. And it wasn't just the food; it was a relaxed Grayson and a stunning sunset. Their conversation turned casual as they ate, washing away the emotional heaviness of the last several minutes.

Grayson went back to being excited about everything, and she was happy to follow him wherever he wanted to go. They got along amazingly well. Too bad it wasn't real, she reminded herself as they finished eating.

"That was the best dinner I've had in a long time," Grayson said, wiping his mouth with a napkin. Then he surprised her by reaching across the table and covering her hand with his. "Thank you, Lexie. Thank you for sharing this with me."

"You're welcome. Grayson, I have to tell you something."

"You can tell me anything, just don't tell me this wasn't fun."

"It was very fun," she said with a smile, meeting his warm gaze.

"I think so, too. You're good for me."

"I don't know if that's true." She licked her lips, knowing the time for truth had arrived. "I need to tell you something about the brownies you ate."

"They were great. In fact, I need better adjectives to describe them: exceptional, superlative, out of this world."

She laughed. "Okay, that's a little much, but I'm glad you liked them. Unfortunately, when I stopped by my aunt's apartment to pick up the brownies, I took the wrong plate. The plate I gave you was supposed to go to my aunt's friend, who is going through chemotherapy."

He gave her a blank look. "I don't understand. Was there something wrong with the brownies? They didn't taste bad."

"My aunt put weed in the brownies so her friend would feel less nauseous. You weren't supposed to get those brownies. You were supposed to get the regular ones." She paused. "You're high, Grayson. That's why you're barefoot and everything is wonderful."

"That's not true. I feel fine. Completely relaxed."

"Exactly. When was the last time you walked barefoot in the sand, talked to seagulls, and ate chili fries?"

He frowned as her words sank in. "Are you saying you drugged me?"

"Not on purpose. I'm sorry. I've been trying to tell you since I found you on the beach, but I didn't think you could hear me or understand what I was saying."

"So, I'm high," he said. "Huh. That does kind of seem right. Because I do like to wear shoes. And I don't usually talk to birds."

"Are you mad?"

"I feel too good and too full to be angry. I might be later," he said honestly. "I don't know. It's hard to say."

"Fair enough. Do you want to walk back?"

He nodded. "I definitely need to walk off the chili."

After throwing away their trash, they grabbed their shoes and started walking back along the beach, the glorious colors of the sunset starting to fade. By the time they got back to Ocean Shores, Grayson's high would be fading, too, and nothing, including her, would seem as amazing as it had before.

But as Grayson took her hand once more, she decided to savor whatever time they had left. They walked in companionable silence, and when they finally made it back to the beach in front of Ocean Shores, the last bit of sun dipped over the horizon.

Grayson stopped near the water's edge. Letting go of her hand, he put his arms around her.

They gazed into each other's eyes for a long minute. "Lexie?"

"Yes," she said breathlessly, knowing what he was asking her.

He leaned down and covered her mouth with his, and she sank into the hot, salty, sexy kiss that completely consumed her. Closing her eyes, she pressed her body closer to his as they kissed again and again as dusk settled over the beach and they lost themselves in each other. She didn't care who else was around, what anyone thought. All she cared about was being with him in this moment, a moment she didn't think she'd ever forget.

Later, she would tell herself it wasn't real, that it was created by her aunt's brownies. But it felt real now, and the connection between them, the chemistry, was unbelievably strong.

She liked this man—too much. She didn't know how it had happened. There were so many reasons why it shouldn't be this way, but it was. And she was loving every second of it.

Of course, it had to end, because they had to breathe, and they had to go inside. They had to go back to being who they were. They stared at each other for a long minute, with unspoken words flowing between them.

And then he took her hand again, and without a word, they walked up the beach, across the path, and into the Ocean Shores complex.

The beautiful silence between them was instantly broken by laughter and talking as the Friday night pool party was in full swing.

Before anyone saw them, Grayson pulled her under the nearby stairwell. "I can't talk to anyone right now, Lexie."

"I understand. I'll tell them you have work to do."

"How many people know I'm high?"

"My aunt, Margaret, and Emmalyn. They were there when Josie realized I'd given you the wrong plate."

He groaned. "Great. So basically everyone."

"Probably by now, yes," she admitted. "I am sorry about the brownies, Grayson. I wanted to do something nice for you, and I messed it up. Don't blame Josie. She told me which plate to take; I just forgot. I wasn't paying attention."

He gave her a small smile. "You're very protective of people: your friends, your aunt, even me. You came looking for me because you thought I might be in trouble."

"I wasn't sure how much you'd eaten or how you were feeling, but yes, I did want to make sure you were all right. And I suspect that your rather low level of anger right now will rise as the high wears off. So I hope you can remember that I'm really sorry."

"That's not what I'm going to remember most, Lexie," he said, gazing into her eyes. He took a quick look around, then planted another brief kiss on her lips. "Goodnight."

"Goodnight. I'll distract everyone while you go up the stairs."

"Thank you."

As they came out from under the stairs, she walked back to the courtyard while he moved up the steps to his apartment. Josie, Margaret, and Frank were at the closest table with Emmalyn and Hunter nearby at the grill.

She fielded all the curious, questioning looks with a smile. "He's fine," she said. "It's all good."

"How angry is he?" Josie asked.

"He's not that mad right now, but I can't guarantee he won't be tomorrow. He really liked your brownies. I think he ate several."

Josie smiled. "Well, I'm glad he's okay. You've been gone a long time. I put your things in your apartment while you were gone."

"Do you want some food?" Emmalyn asked. "We have extra chicken."

"No, thanks, I already ate. I'm tired. We walked on the beach for a long time, so I'm going to call it a night. I'll see you tomorrow."

She made her way around the pool and into her apartment, entering with a sigh of both relief and a little bit of yearning. Maybe if she'd waited to tell Grayson about the brownies, they would have ended up in his apartment together. But that would have been a bad idea, she told herself forcefully. She couldn't take advantage of the man, and she didn't want to be with him when he wasn't in his right mind.

But she did want to be with him, and she had no idea how she would get through the next two weeks without thinking about how that might possibly happen. However, she knew that once Grayson was fully in control of his senses, his logical, practical business mind would determine that a personal relationship with her would be a conflict of interest, and he would shut that idea down immediately. He might even leave before his month was up. She might never see him again, and that thought was more overwhelming than her usual nightmare of having her home sold out from under her. The worst thing was that she felt absolutely powerless to do anything about either one of them.

And as she flopped down on the couch in despair, she really wished she had kept some of Josie's brownies for herself.

CHAPTER THIRTEEN

Lexie had spent Saturday shooting a wedding and wondering if Grayson remembered everything he'd done, everything he'd said, or if the night was a big blank. When her phone had buzzed with a text from him at five o'clock Saturday evening, her heart had nearly stopped.

Can you be ready to leave for Joshua Tree by 10 AM tomorrow? Have a meeting at a property at 12:30. Still interested in going?

She'd stared at the message for a full minute before typing back: *Yes! Absolutely.*

His response had been immediate: *Good. See you tomorrow.*

No mention of Friday night. No reference to the brownies or their conversation at Chuck's Chili, just businesslike efficiency that could have meant anything—that he was fine with what happened, or that he was so uncomfortable he wanted to pretend it never occurred.

Now, standing in front of her bathroom mirror Sunday morning, she applied sunscreen and tried to manage her expectations for the trip. Grayson was a man who kept his word. He'd told her he would take her to Joshua Tree, and he might just be fulfilling a commitment he'd made before she'd drugged him.

Whatever the reason, she had a chance to spend time with

him, and she was going to take it. She also would have an opportunity to photograph one of the more interesting locations in Southern California, so it was a win-win. At least, she hoped so. She still didn't know how Grayson felt about his unexpected high now that he was sober, but when a knock came at the door, she knew she was about to find out.

She opened the door and gave him a smile, her gut clenching at the sight of him. He wore tan slacks and a cream-colored polo shirt, looking unfairly handsome in the morning light.

"Ready to go?" he asked with a smile that seemed genuine.

"Absolutely." She grabbed her purse and her camera bag, then locked the door behind her. "I'm glad you still wanted to go."

"Of course," he said as they walked out to the parking lot.

She was a little relieved there was no one else around. Not that this trip was a secret, but she'd been generating a lot of gossip since the brownie incident.

Sliding into the passenger seat of his car, she fastened her seat belt and let out a little sigh.

He gave her a questioning look as he started the engine. "What was that sigh about?"

"Just relieved we didn't run into anyone. I've been getting a lot of questions..."

"Got it," he said as he pulled out of the lot. "I've been getting a lot of curious looks, but the only person who was brave enough to ask me about my experience with the brownies was Kaia."

"I told her not to say anything."

"I'm not sure she knows how to not say something," he said dryly.

"What did you tell her?"

"That all I could remember was a fun walk on the beach and some great chili fries."

"Is that all you can remember?"

He shot her a look. "No. I remember the rest of it, Lexie. It all has a bit of a hazy glow, but I know what we did, and I know how I felt."

"You were a much more cheerful version of yourself."

"Apparently, I get happy when I get high."

She laughed. "Was that the first time for you?"

"It was," he admitted. "I've never done any drugs. Too busy studying or working. Plus, I like to be in control."

"That makes sense. I'm sorry I inadvertently took that control away from you."

"Stop. We're not doing this for the next two hours. You already apologized. So did your aunt. It was an honest mistake. And when you knew I was in trouble, you came to find me and you stayed with me."

"That wasn't hard. You were pretty funny, especially when you were talking to the seagull."

A smile lifted his lips as he stopped at a light and their gazes met once more. "While I do remember what we did, I don't remember everything I said. Hopefully, it wasn't too embarrassing."

"It wasn't. You just used a lot of superlatives. It was fun to see you unguarded, open, not thinking about what you said before you said it."

"Is that how you see me?" he asked curiously. "As someone guarded, closed off, deliberate in what I say?"

"Yes," she said honestly. "You don't see yourself that way?"

He didn't answer immediately, then said, "I don't like to think of myself that way, but I can't say you're wrong. I grew up with parents who weren't that interested in what I had to say. When I was a kid, I loved to read, and I liked to tell my parents about my books, but my mother would be bored within sixty seconds, and my father would cut me off and say he wanted to hear all about it but maybe another time. Eventually, I realized there wasn't really any point to trying to share my books with them."

"That's kind of sad, but I can also relate. I learned early on that I'd get more attention if I liked the things my parents liked. With my mom, it was clothes, makeup, jewelry, and workouts.

With my dad, it was the law. When I gave that up, he and I had nothing to talk about, and while my mom still keeps in touch, she also doesn't really care about photography or Ocean Shores or my aunt Josie. Since I'm not around to shop with her, our conversations are very short. Plus, she feels like she has to take my dad's side. And he thinks I'm throwing my life away, so she doesn't want to support that."

"You're not throwing anything away. You're following your passion."

"I thought I was doing that, but I wasn't fully committed to taking the real leap into the unknown. Instead, I filled my days with jobs to make money. I've always been practical. I was raised to understand that work is about money, so it didn't feel right to not do anything to make money. To that end, I filled up my day with jobs I told myself were side gigs, but they took over all my time. Strangely enough, you were the first person to actually call that out. I'm sure my friends probably wondered what I was doing, but no one came right out and asked me."

"Is that your way of saying thank you?" he asked with a note of humor in his voice.

"I suppose. Anyway, I feel like I'm getting onto the right track. I was talking to Josie about it the other day. She's always been the one person in my family I can speak to without guarding my words, and she's incredibly supportive. Of course, she also walked away from a very lucrative career, so she can understand why I did the same."

"Why did she walk away?" he asked curiously. "She won an Oscar. That seems pretty incredible."

"She's never really told me the whole story. She just said she felt used and betrayed by people in her circle: her husband, her agent, and her friends. I think there might have been infidelity and a love triangle, but those were just rumors I read when I looked online to see what had been written about her. At any rate, she told me there came a point when she felt like her entire life was make-believe, and she wanted to live in a world that was real, where people didn't lie or pretend. So, she left Hollywood. I guess she traveled around for a few months before she made it to Oceanside. She rented an apartment at Ocean Shores, and she's been there ever since. Thirty-five years. It's a long time, Grayson."

"I'm aware," he said shortly.

"I don't want to talk about the possible sale," she added. "I just want to say one thing, and then we'll change the subject. Ocean Shores gave my aunt a family and friends. Even people who have come and gone over the years stay in touch with her. They send her photos of their kids, of their children's wedding, of their first grandbaby. The community isn't a static thing. It changes as people need more space and move on, but while they're there, it's everything. And even after they leave, they keep in touch." She took a quick breath, wanting to get it all out before she had to shut up. "When I first moved in after I left my law job, I was really spinning, not sure I'd made the right decision. Most of my friends were still lawyers and still in LA, so I didn't really have anyone to talk to, but I found even better friends in the building. Anyway, that's all I'm going to say about it for now."

"For now," he echoed.

"Well, I can't promise forever."

"I know. And, Lexie..." He glanced over at her. "I heard you."

"Okay. Good. So, you said you used to love to talk about books. What are you reading right now?"

"You don't want to hear about my current read," he said with a laugh.

"I really do. I like to talk about books. I'm even in a book club with some of the women in the building. Although we tend to drink more wine than chat about the book at our meetings, but I still read. So, what's on your nightstand?"

"A twelve-hundred-page book titled *The Power Broker* about Robert Moses, who was in power in New York for over forty years and shaped the development of the city. It's his biography, but there's so much incredible information about the time period, the backroom deals, and how politics played out in the local and state government. It's fascinating."

"Wow. You're an overachiever even in your choice of books. Twelve hundred pages?"

"Something like that," he said. "It's a doorstop, but it's fascinating."

"How long will it take you to read it?"

"Probably a month or more. I don't have a lot of time to read. But it's very well-written. The author puts you right into the story. I feel like I know Robert Moses. I know the people he's dealing with."

"Does it inspire you for your own work since you are selling and buying buildings and are a part of the development community?"

"It's inspiring, but it also makes me wary. There were a lot of shady deals going on back then, and I'm sure there are just as many now. It reminds me to be on my guard. Now, your turn. What's on your nightstand?"

"A mystery thriller about a woman who marries a man and then he disappears on their wedding night. She has no idea who he really is or was."

"Sounds interesting."

"It's a page-turner. I was reading it last night and stayed up way too late to finish a chapter. I'm almost done, and I think I know who the villain is, but I'm not quite sure, and that's my favorite kind of story when I don't really know what's happening, even though I think I do. It's fun. What's the first book you ever read?"

As Grayson told her about the first book he remembered making an impact on his life, she settled into her seat, eager to know more about him, even if it was just what he liked to read. He seemed to feel the same way, and for the next hour, they chatted about everything under the sun.

He liked basketball because it was fast-paced and fortunes

could change in an instant. She told him there was nothing better than a day at the ballpark with a foot-long hot dog smothered in mustard and relish and the sun beating down on the field, the players battling to get a hit when most of the time they didn't.

They also talked about music and movies, their worst first dates, and their best memories from their childhood. They actually had a lot in common when it came to family. They were both only children. They both had fathers who were brilliantly successful and driven and mothers who had created separate passions for themselves, but at the end of the day were still happiest in their roles as corporate wives.

She wondered if Grayson would end up with someone like that, someone who knew his world and would be good at hosting client dinners and managing a big house. And she found herself asking that very question, a little surprised when the words came out, but she was curious.

"I haven't really thought about marriage," he said. "I'm thirty-three. I have plenty of time."

"But you must date, right? Do you have a girlfriend?"

"If I did, I wouldn't have kissed you," he said pointedly. "What about you? You're not seeing anyone, are you?"

"No. Same answer you just gave me." She paused. "Have you had any serious relationships?"

"I'm not sure how you define serious. I've dated off and on. Some were relationships that lasted several months, but nothing beyond that. Frankly, I find relationships to be a lot of pressure, and I have preferred to focus on business, especially with my dad wanting to hand off pieces of it to me. I have to be at the top of my game. And I don't want to worry about disappointing someone because I'm taking a late meeting."

"That makes sense. But at some point, you'll want more than business."

"Probably," he conceded. "When was your last relationship?"

"It ended right before I came here two years ago. My

boyfriend was also a lawyer, and he could not understand how I could walk away from my dad's firm when I was going to be on the fast track up the ladder. He didn't support me at all. In fact, I started to realize that maybe he was more interested in attaching himself to my fast track than he was in having a loving relationship with me."

"Sounds like you avoided a land mine."

"I think so. Since then, I've dated but I haven't met anyone I really connected with." She took a breath, making sure she didn't add the final two words that were hovering on her lips: *until now.* Because they weren't dating, and while they had an undeniable chemistry and what she considered to be a pretty strong connection, they were definitely on different paths.

As a somewhat awkward silence fell between them, she knew she needed to change the subject. "Tell me about this building we're going to see."

"It's a vintage motel in Palm Desert, built in the nineteen twenties when the Hollywood stars would head to the desert in the winter. In fact, I think a bunch of stars stayed there back in the day. It's, of course, completely run-down now, but the bones are good, and I think I could give it a new life."

"By renovating it? Or would you tear it down and build a luxury apartment building?"

"Actually, I was thinking about turning it into a development with a mix of affordable housing and retail space."

"When you say affordable housing, what exactly do you mean? Is that like three units are affordable and the rest are not?"

"No. The land the property sits on is quite large. We could have two buildings, and the first floor of each building could be affordable housing, and the upper two floors would be market price. The ratio would be about thirty percent, which I realize could be better, but I also have to pay for what I want to do."

"I understand. It's good that you even want to do affordable housing. So many builders don't."

"To be honest, it's probably going to be required by the city, so I'm not being that generous. Maybe I could improve the percentage to fifty-fifty. It's just an idea at this point. I've seen the property in photographs but not in person. Once I'm walking around, I'll know more about what I can do and what I want to do. At the end of the day, it might not be the right project for my company. My father isn't that excited about it. He thinks the desert is a harsh environment, and with summer temperatures into the 120s at times, the cost of utilities will be high. It's also not centrally located to the music events and tennis tournament, so there are things to consider." He gave her an apologetic look. "Sorry if I'm boring you."

"I'm not bored at all."

"You're being nice."

"No. I just like getting to know you, and it's fun to go on a road trip."

"It is fun," he agreed. "I don't usually look at my property evaluations as road trips, but this one is different. Have you done your research on Joshua Tree?"

"I have. But like you, I think I'll have even better ideas when I actually get there."

"Well, my part of this trip won't take too long."

"It can take as long as it needs to take, Grayson. I'll support you just as you're supporting me. That's what friends do."

"Friends, huh?" he muttered. "Never thought you'd call me your friend, Lexie. I'm not sure I like it."

"Because you'd rather be my enemy?" she asked in surprise.

He shot her a hot look. "Because I might want to be more than your friend."

She shivered at the intensity of his gaze, the shocking bluntness of his words.

"I shouldn't have said that," he muttered, looking away. "I don't know why I did."

She didn't know why he had said the words, either, but she was happy to know she wasn't alone in the way she was feeling.

But she also didn't know what to do about it, and he didn't seem to know, either.

―――

As Grayson pulled into the parking lot of the Desert Palms Motor Lodge, he almost wished it had taken them longer than two hours to get there, because he'd enjoyed talking to Lexie. The conversation had flowed fast and easy through most of the trip, until he'd created an awkward tension between them, but hopefully they would get past that. And he couldn't worry about that now. It was time to get down to business.

The lodge sat like a time capsule in the desert sun, its pink stucco walls and turquoise trim faded and dirty, probably from many a desert dust storm whipping up the dirt lots on either side of the property.

As he stepped out of the car, the heat hit him hard, already nearing eighty degrees.

"It's hot," Lexie commented as she came around the front of the car. "We are definitely in the desert, and this place has seen better days. But like you said, there's an old Hollywood kind of vibe to it." She paused as a white SUV pulled into the parking lot, and a tall, thin blonde, wearing a short, sleeveless dress got out of the car.

"Is that the agent?" Lexie asked. "She looks like a movie star."

"Yes," he said as Paula Conroy walked over to greet them. She had a leather bag slung over her shoulder and a thick folder in her hand.

"Sorry, I'm late, Mr. Holt."

"That's fine. This is Lexie Price."

"Nice to meet you," Paula said with a cool smile in Lexie's direction. "Have you looked around?"

"Not yet. We just got here."

"Then I'll show you around. Follow me. I'll show you the pool area first."

She led them through an iron gate that was swinging on one rusty hinge into a large area with palm trees still swaying above the empty swimming pool. There were old barbecues and picnic tables under a broken-down wooden canopy, as well as a large grassy area that was overgrown with weeds.

"Back in the day," Paula continued, "they used to show movies on that wall." She pointed to the white wall, which was the back side of the building. "The grass was trimmed. The barbecues were smoking. The bar area was active, and drinks were being served to all the guests. Of course, that was like sixty years ago, but there are still some people who remember this place in its prime." She took a breath as her phone rang. "Excuse me for one minute. I have to take this."

As Paula moved away to take her call, he looked at Lexie, who was wandering around the area and was now staring at the big white wall, actually not so white anymore. "What do you think?" he asked as he joined her.

"The possibilities are endless. I like the image of movies being shown outdoors. What if you incorporated a small outdoor theater into your plans? It would be a fun and interesting addition, and unlike anything most apartment complexes have. And if you're going to have kids as residents, maybe a play yard over there," she said, pointing to a weed-filled area. "Or you could have an organic garden and let the tenants plant what they want. That could be beautiful."

He loved the way her creative mind worked, seeing the potential of something old and run-down and not thinking it should be demolished, but restored and turned into something incredible.

"But you probably have your own ideas," she said as she ran out of breath. "Sorry to ramble on like that."

"I asked you what you thought, and your ideas are good. You have a way of looking at the world that's rather unique."

"Would you mind if I took a few photos? I think this place could provide some intriguing shots. But I need to get my camera out of the car."

He tossed her the keys. "Go for it."

While Lexie went back to the car to grab her camera, Paula rejoined him.

"Sorry about that," she said. "Do you want to take a look at the other side of the property? I do have a key to inside the building, but there's not much to see."

"Let's take a peek anyway." For the next twenty minutes, he checked out every inch of the property, his own imagination firing up with ideas. He caught glimpses of Lexie shooting pictures of the front of the building, the broken-down sign, and the old, rusted fountain that probably hadn't worked in fifty years.

Paula talked about price per square foot and what else was happening on the adjoining properties and then launched into a sales pitch. He'd heard most of it before and appreciated her enthusiasm, but he would still need to run the numbers himself.

"I think I'm good," he said finally. "Thanks for meeting me."

"Happy to do it," Paula replied. "And I hope to hear from you soon."

"I'll be in touch." He caught up with Lexie at the car. She looked hot and flushed in her sleeveless top and jeans, but her eyes were bright with energy and enthusiasm.

"We can go," he said, opening the car door. "I don't know about you, but I'm ready for some air-conditioning."

"More than ready."

As they got into the car, he lowered the temperature and cranked up the fan, then pulled out of the parking spot. "Next stop, Joshua Tree."

CHAPTER FOURTEEN

As he drove away from the lodge, he turned to Lexie. "Are you hungry? Do you want to stop for lunch?"

"I am hungry, but I'm eager to get to Joshua Tree. It's a very large park, from what I've read. Maybe we could pick up some sandwiches on the way."

"That sounds good."

She pulled out her phone. "I'll see what I can find."

As she researched food options, he turned onto the highway, impressed by the jagged brown ridges of the mountains surrounding them. They looked both desolate and majestic. He hadn't spent a lot of time in the desert, but he did like the landscape.

"I found a gourmet deli," Lexie said a few minutes later. "It's right outside the entrance to the Joshua Tree National Park. We can eat and then explore."

"Perfect." He turned on some music as she settled back in her seat, her gaze also on the horizon. There was so much emptiness around them, but also a lot to look at. Or maybe it was just that he had time to look, and he hadn't taken the time for a road trip in...he couldn't remember when. His travels were always from point A to point B with a purposeful goal for every stop and usually a tight timetable.

Although they had a schedule today, it felt different. His business was done. This next stop was purely for Lexie, and he was looking forward to every minute of it. It wasn't just because of the interesting sights she'd already told him about wanting to see; it was because of her.

She'd asked him earlier if he'd thought about marriage and what kind of woman he would want in his life, and he'd said he hadn't been focusing on relationships but on business. But it was also because he'd never met anyone who made him think about a long-term relationship. But the free-spirited photographer sitting next to him was making him reconsider a lot of things about his life.

She was on her own journey to a new identity but seeing her struggle with whether she'd taken a big enough leap forward, had made him think more about his own journey.

He'd always known he would go to work for his father and had started in the company with a summer job in high school. Through college, grad school, and then in his twenties, his father had made sure he spent time in every department. After he'd turned thirty, more responsibility had come his way. Now, three years later, his father was talking about making him the CEO while he became chairman of the board and stepped away from the day-to-day business operations.

That title and that job had been his goal for years, which was why he had put in so many hours, why he kept trying to bring in new business to prove to his father he wasn't just taking what he was given, but he was also growing the company. That intense business focus had made his life narrow, his stress level high, and his ability to relax and enjoy a moment almost impossible. It wasn't until his father had sent him to Ocean Shores that he'd taken time to breathe, to look around, to see something else...someone else.

He couldn't stop himself from looking over at Lexie. She met his gaze and gave him a happy smile, and he felt that same warm feeling of joy run through his body. They'd started out as enemies, but she didn't feel like his enemy. Nor did she feel exactly like his friend, not after the way they'd kissed each other. But what did that make them?

Her smile faded, and she gave him a questioning look. "Are you okay? Are you tired of driving? I'm happy to take over."

"No, I'm good. I was just thinking about something else."

"Something that put a frown on your face. What was it?"

He definitely could not tell her, so he settled on a half-truth and told her what he'd been thinking before he'd looked at her. "I've been so busy the last few years I haven't taken time to do things like this."

"Well, it's good that you're going now. But for me, it's also a job, not just a look around."

"I know. I didn't mean it that way. I don't want you to think I'm not taking your work seriously."

"I don't think that. You're actually surprisingly supportive."

"Why surprisingly?"

"I don't know. Because you thrive on business and deal-making and love the kind of corporate world I left."

"It might not have been right for you, but that doesn't mean it's not right for me."

"Do you love what you do?" she asked curiously.

"For the most part."

"And the other part?"

"Well, it is work," he said. "Does anyone love everything about their job?"

"You're right. Work has its ups and downs. But you do seem particularly driven, and you've admitted as much to me. Is it about proving something to your dad? To yourself? Or is it just about making the most money you could possibly make?"

"It's all of that. I don't want anyone to think I'm running the company because I was born into it. I want to have the same respect my father had and perhaps even more. I want to grow the company. I want it to be even better than it has been."

"Why does it have to be better?" she challenged.

His frown returned. "I don't know. Because it does. Everyone wants to make their mark. I'm sure you're not aiming to take less-than-amazing photographs. You want yours to be better than everyone else's."

"I don't think of it that way. I want the pictures to be good, but mostly I want them to be a representation of how I see the world. I want to expose people to places they've never seen. But I don't think about being the best photographer in the world. I just want to be really good at what I do."

"So do I."

"But you also want to be better than your dad." She gave him a smile of understanding. "I actually understand that, Grayson, because I had that feeling when I worked with my father. I felt a pressure to prove to him that I was worthy of following in his footsteps. But the truth is, I wasn't as good as him, because I didn't love it as much as he did. I know it's different for you, because you enjoy what you do. But maybe…" She paused for a moment, then said, "Maybe what's most important is that you make the company yours when you take it over. That could mean bigger and better, or maybe it means you take a turn in direction. You do what you want to do. That's really what you've been working for. The opportunity to call your own shots. When your father retires and you're fully in charge, you should be running a company that you're proud of, whether it's one your father would have wanted to run or not."

He gave her a thoughtful look before turning his gaze back to the road. Her words echoed around in his head for a long minute. "You're right. I wasn't looking at it that way, but I should because my father and I are different people."

"If he respects you enough to hand over his company to you, he'll respect whatever you do after that."

"I'm not completely sure that's true. He has trouble giving up control. He tells me another year, and he'll be done. But I don't know if that year will turn into two or three."

"Would you ever think about starting your own company?"

"I would," he admitted. "It has crossed my mind, especially when my father annoys me with odd requests."

"Like living at Ocean Shores for a month?"

"Exactly." He gave her another quick look. "But I'm not mad about that anymore."

"Why not?"

"Because I'm actually starting to have a good time."

She smiled. "Let's try to keep that going."

———

Lexie was happy to hear that Grayson was having a good time and loved that he'd confided in her about his job, his aspirations. She liked knowing what made him tick, and she was also happy that they still had some fun times ahead. Being away from Ocean Shores felt like an escape from the dark cloud hanging over the future, something she refused to think about now. She just wanted to stay in the moment, because it was a damn good moment.

A short time later, they reached the small town of Joshua Tree, which boasted a Main Street filled with touristy shops, cafés, art galleries, and even an old-time saloon. The gourmet deli was at the end of the street. The heat was even more oppressive, but the inside of the deli was cool and clean. She ordered a tuna salad while Grayson opted for a triple-decker club sandwich, and when their food came, she couldn't help but steal a few of his fries.

"You don't mind, do you?" she asked.

"What's mine is yours," he said with a smile. "But I had you pegged for a woman who boldly ordered her own fries, even if she was opting for a salad."

"I usually do, but I was thinking I was hot, and a salad would be less heavy. However, these are delicious."

"Take as many as you want. They were generous with the fries."

"You know, I had you pegged for a man who was more comfortable in restaurants with linens and crystal glasses and more than one fork in the place setting. Friday night, I saw you eat chili fries with onions and cheese and thought that was just because you were high, but now I'm thinking you actually like French fries."

"I love them. And I don't care about linen tablecloths and crystal glasses. What I care most about is if the food is good."

"But you wouldn't entertain your clients at Chuck's Chili or this place, would you?"

"No, I wouldn't. Because our clients expect me to treat them like they're important and deserving of only the best."

"My father felt the same way. He always treated his big clients to luxurious dinners, trips, and box seats to sporting events. I know he had fun doing it, because who wouldn't have fun? But it seemed like a lot of money was going toward people who did not need it. And trust me when I say, I am not against having money. I like it just as much as anyone. I just don't want to do certain things to get it. In my case, that was being a lawyer. Now, I'll probably be a starving artist who turned up her nose at being a wedding photographer."

"But you'll be happy."

"If I'm not, I'll do something else. One thing I have realized is that nothing has to be finite. Life has twists and turns, and different paths make the journey more interesting."

"Did you make that up, or did you read it in a book?" he teased.

She laughed. "I don't think I read it, but maybe. Things have a way of sticking in my head."

"Well, I like it," he said with a nod. "You can't be disappointed if you end up somewhere different than you expected."

"Because it might be better," she finished, her body tingling as his warm gaze swept across her face. And she couldn't help wondering if maybe his journey to sell Ocean Shores could take a left turn, but she didn't want to get into that now. "Are you done? Shall we go?"

"Let's do it."

When they arrived at the park entrance, Grayson rolled down his window, fed bills into the automated kiosk, and grabbed a park map from the dispenser.

"Here," he said, handing her the map once they were moving again.

"Look at all these places," she said, unfolding it. "Hidden Valley, Skull Rock, Cholla Cactus Garden... the names alone sound like poetry."

"Where do you want to start?"

"Everywhere," she said with a laugh. "But let's see what calls to us."

Entering the park felt like entering another world, Lexie thought, sitting up straighter, her breath catching in her chest as Grayson drove them past the first grouping of Joshua trees.

"They don't look like trees," she murmured. "More like monsters with spiky arms, in strange poses, each one different from the other. They almost look like they could come alive, don't they?"

"Yeah, like the trees in a nightmare," he said, pulling off to a vista point.

She jumped out of the car with her camera, taking pictures of the trees from far away before getting closer. She glanced back to see Grayson leaning against the hood of the car, watching her.

"Take your time," he said. "We're in no rush."

She loved that he was willing to let her take whatever time she needed because her creative juices were flowing, and she wanted to find the perfect angles to show different views of the trees.

After almost thirty minutes, she headed back to the car, and they drove deeper into the park, the road curving between granite boulders that rose like giant sculptures from the ground. They stopped next at Hidden Valley, and as she got out of the car to take in the scene, she was mesmerized by the beauty of the rock walls that cupped the valley, the way the sunlight struck the stone, turning it into a canvas of gold and amber.

As they moved down the Hidden Valley trail, they found themselves walking behind a young family—parents with a maybe-five-year-old boy who stopped every few feet to examine rocks, lizards, or anything else that caught his attention.

"Look, Daddy! This rock looks like a dinosaur!"

"It does, buddy. What kind of dinosaur do you think?" the father said.

The boy launched into an elaborate explanation involving a T. Rex and something called a "super-mega-saurus" while his parents listened with patient attention, asking follow-up questions that encouraged his imagination. She noticed something wistful cross Grayson's face as he watched their easy interaction, and as they continued past the group, she wondered what personal memories the moment had stirred.

"Sweet family," she commented. "And a very talkative kid."

"Yeah." He was quiet for a moment. "My parents would have probably hired someone with paleontology credentials to explain dinosaurs to me."

"That sounds... thorough. But kind of sad."

He shrugged. "Some parents are hands-on; some are not."

"Did you like dinosaurs?"

"What child doesn't like the magic of a dinosaur story?" he returned.

She smiled, catching a glimpse of the boy he'd once been.

"But I don't think we're going to find any dinosaur bones here."

"I wouldn't be so sure about that. This place is pretty magical."

He smiled. "I guess we'll find out."

As they moved down the trail, her interest was drawn to an outcropping of rocks. She climbed onto one of the smaller boulders and knelt, her hair falling in her face as she adjusted the settings on her camera. Then she aimed the lens upward, framing the rocks above her against the sky. When she was done, she turned back to Grayson. "This is so stunningly beautiful."

"I agree," he said as he snapped a photo with his phone, which happened to be aimed at her.

"Did you just take my picture?" she asked in surprise.

"Maybe."

"With all this magnificence around us, that's the photo you wanted to take?"

He gazed back at her. "Absolutely."

A tingle ran down her spine. "You're crazy."

"I'm not. I want you to see what you look like when you're doing what you love."

"Well, thanks," she said. "But you should take photos of the scenery."

"I don't need to because I'll see yours, and they'll be better."

"I hope so. I don't know if I can do this place justice. Maybe I'm not that good."

"You are that good, and remember what you said before, as long as you love what you're doing, it's all good."

"You're right. Let's go back to the car and drive to the cactus garden."

As they headed back to their vehicle, they passed by the family once more, and the kid was still talking about dinosaurs. After sliding into the passenger seat, she checked the map and directed Grayson to the cactus garden, which was a ten-minute drive through canopies of trees that continued to make her feel like she'd been transported into another dimension.

They parked near the entrance to the garden and followed

the short loop trail to see the chollas, which were called "teddy bear cactus" for their deceptively fuzzy appearance. But each spiny creature was its own unique creation and glowed like it was lit by the desert sun. It was quiet here, with only the whisper of wind through the cactus spines and the occasional call of a desert bird. It made every sound more significant: the crunch of gravel under their feet, the click of her camera.

As she crouched to frame a shot of the densest patch of chollas with the distant mountains behind them, she noticed a young girl nearby, maybe ten, struggling with a small digital camera while her mother chased a toddler nearby. The girl kept taking the same shot of a particularly large cholla over and over, frowning at the results.

"Try moving over there, closer to that smaller one," she suggested, pointing to a spot where a smaller cactus created better foreground interest. "Sometimes getting closer to something in front makes the whole picture in the back more interesting."

The girl brightened and moved to the suggested spot. When she looked at her camera screen this time, her face lit up. "That's so much better! Thank you!"

"You're welcome."

The girl beamed and ran off to show her mother.

"That was nice of you," Grayson commented.

"I just wanted her to get the best shot," she said with a shrug. "There's nothing better than that moment when you finally capture what you were trying to see."

"You do that a lot—help people without thinking much about it."

His words surprised her. "Do I?"

"You see things differently. Not just through the lens—in life. You put yourself forward, you reach out, you don't hang back, waiting for someone else to jump in." He gave her a smile. "You're as unique as these cacti."

"But not as prickly."

"Sometimes," he said with a laugh.

She grinned back at him. "You were being so complimentary a second ago... Let's keep walking. I think the ridge is only about a mile from here, and I don't want to get back in the car yet."

"Sounds good to me."

As the trail took them into the hills of the park, the air cooled, and a faint breeze picked up as the sun began to sink toward the tall peaks to the west. It was almost five now. She couldn't believe how much time they'd spent in the park, but she still wasn't ready to leave. When they reached the ridge, they found themselves looking out over the beautiful Coachella Valley surrounded by the rocky mountain landscape.

"I thought the sunset over the ocean would be impossible to beat, but this view has its own beauty," she murmured as Grayson's shoulder brushed against hers.

"Don't you want to take a photo?" he asked.

She shook her head. "I have enough. I want to take a minute to just be in the picture instead of behind the camera." As she glanced at him, his expression grew serious. And there was a look in his eyes that she couldn't quite decipher. "What are you thinking?"

"That when I kissed you on the beach the other night, I didn't think I could have picked a better setting." He reached out and tucked a strand of hair behind her ear, his thumb brushing her cheek as he slid it down her face. "But it feels like we should see how this setting compares."

He was so handsome in the late afternoon light, his thick dark hair falling over his forehead, his cheeks warmed by the sun, his lips ever so inviting... She wanted to kiss him more than she wanted to take her next breath, and when he didn't make a move, she did.

Cupping his face with her hands, she pressed her body against his as she kissed his lips, and as he wrapped his arms around her, she sank deeper into his embrace. She felt so connected to him. Every taste, every touch, was better than the last. When they finally broke apart, she looked up at him and said, "Well? How did it compare?"

"The scorecard doesn't go that high," he murmured, his hands lingering at her waist. "I've never met anyone like you, Lexie."

"Same," she said, but she couldn't help wishing that the reason they'd met was not because he wanted to sell her home. And just like that, the dark cloud was back. "We should go. We still have to walk back to the car."

He nodded, but there was reluctance in his gaze. "All right, but I'm going to hang on to this," he said, taking her hand in his. "Just in case the path gets rocky."

She had a feeling their path was always going to be rocky, and there was going to come a time when he would let go, but that time was not now.

They arrived at the car thirty minutes later and as they drove out of the park and down the highway, she was glad that the light was fading. She might need the shadows to hide from herself, from her growing feelings for the man beside her, a man she'd probably never see again in two weeks. But she wasn't going to think about that now.

Twenty minutes later, as they were nearing the turnoff for the highway that would lead them through the mountains and back to Ocean Shores, traffic came to a crashing halt with lights, fire engines, and police cars blocking the exit.

"What's going on?" she asked.

"Looks like some kind of bad accident," he muttered. "This isn't good."

They barely moved for the next ten minutes, and they had no idea what was going on because there were several trucks in front of them, blocking the view.

Finally, the traffic started to move a few feet at a time. When they got to the exit, they saw it blocked off by orange cones. She rolled down her window to hear one police officer talking to another about the road being closed for the foreseeable future.

Grayson put their destination into the GPS as they were forced to move down the highway. "Any other way to the coast is going to add a couple of hours to our trip," he said.

"Do we have a choice?"

He didn't say anything for a few minutes, then said, "We could find a hotel, spend the night, get up early, and drive back in the morning."

Her heart began to race. "I guess that's an option."

"Do you have to be anywhere early tomorrow?"

"No. I'm doing a family portrait at four, but I don't have anything before that. I'll look something up."

She ran through the local options. "The closest place is back in Joshua Tree."

"Then we'll go back."

She gave him the address, and he got off at the next exit and circled back around. They hit more traffic as they neared the exit from the opposite direction, but they weren't delayed too long. Several minutes later, they arrived at the Rustic Cottages, which was a bed-and-breakfast with a main house and several small cabins tucked in the surrounding trees.

The office at the Rustic Cottages was decorated with vintage desert memorabilia and staffed by a friendly woman with silver hair and kind eyes.

"You're in luck," she said. "I have one cabin left. Queen bed, private bath, little kitchenette. It's our nicest one, actually."

"One cabin?" Lexie asked.

"I'm afraid that's all I have. We've just checked in some folks who can't get home because of the accident."

"That's why we're here, too," she said.

"Well, we're happy to have you. We have drinks and snacks in the dining room now. Breakfast in the morning runs from seven to ten." She reached into a drawer. "And since you don't have any luggage, here's our overnight kit. Toothbrushes, toothpaste, and a few other items you might need."

"Thanks," she said. "This is very nice of you."

"It's nothing. I hope you enjoy your stay." She handed them a key. "It's the first cottage on your left. But feel free to grab some drinks and snacks before you go."

As she took the key, she turned to Grayson. "Let's check out the dining room."

He smiled. "We should have found somewhere to eat dinner."

"I'm not that hungry, but I wouldn't mind a little something."

The dining room had a bigger spread than she'd expected. She poured herself a glass of wine and filled a plate with cheese and crackers, fresh berries, and a chocolate chip cookie. Grayson also grabbed a plate, and she couldn't help but smile when he bypassed the brownies for a cookie.

He met her gaze and grinned. "It wouldn't be as good," he said as they sat down at a small table.

"Look, there's a chessboard," she said, pointing to the set between them. "Do you know how to play?"

"I do. Do you?"

"As a matter of fact, I do. My father loves chess. What do you think about a game?"

"Sounds good," he said.

She was relieved to have something to do to postpone going into that very small cabin with the queen bed. She knew Grayson would be the perfect gentleman. She just didn't know if she wanted him to be.

CHAPTER FIFTEEN

They ate their snacks and sipped wine as the chessboard between them turned into a battleground. Lexie wanted badly to win, but Grayson was proving a ruthless opponent—calm, calculated, and infuriatingly clever. Every time she thought she'd set a trap, he slipped around it with maddening ease.

She told herself she was just dragging out the game because she loved a challenge, but the truth was more dangerous. Thinking about the night ahead and sharing a tiny cabin with him was giving her far too many reckless ideas, and as long as there were pawns on the board, she could pretend strategy mattered more than attraction.

But it didn't. Not when her pulse jumped every time his dark eyes flicked up to hers. Not when she knew he might be the man who took away her home, her aunt's home, her friends' homes. Wanting him felt like playing straight into a checkmate.

"You've been staring at the board for five minutes," he said. "That's the longest you've ever taken. Which means you've realized I'm about to crush you."

She arched a brow. "Crush me? That's a little dramatic."

"Checkmate is checkmate. Might as well accept your fate." He leaned back, smug confidence radiating off him.

Her fingers tightened on her rook. "I don't quit."

"I've noticed." His gaze lingered, sharp enough that she felt it in her chest. "So what's taking you so long? It's not like you to hesitate."

She forced a shrug, though her pulse was thumping. "Maybe I'm plotting something brilliant."

"Or maybe you're stalling because you know you're cornered."

The words landed with an edge of truth—about the game and everything else between them. She slid a pawn forward, not her best move, but it bought her time.

"See?" he said, smoothly capturing it with his bishop. "You can fight me all you want, Lexie, but sooner or later, I win."

She wished she found his cocky attitude unattractive, but she didn't. Because she knew he just loved a good battle, and she would give him one. "We'll see about that."

They sparred another twenty minutes, each move more desperate than strategic on her part, until finally her king was trapped.

"Damn," she muttered.

"Do you concede?"

"I really don't want to, but I guess I don't have a choice."

"So, I win."

"Okay, you win," she said. "But I made you work for it."

"You did," he agreed. His eyes gleamed with satisfaction. "Which makes the victory sweeter." He paused, looking around the room. "I think the wine party is over."

"They probably want to clean up. We should go."

As they made their way through the lobby, they said goodnight to the woman at the front desk and then left the building in search of their cabin. It was only about ten feet away, which was far closer than she'd been hoping for.

She put the key in the lock and opened the door. The cabin was definitely cozy and rustic, but also warm and inviting with knotty pine walls and a colorful throw rug on the hardwood floor. The bathroom was clean and updated, and the kitchenette was just a counter with a hot plate and a small refrigerator. In the middle of everything was one queen bed that seemed to dominate the space.

"I'll sleep on the floor," Grayson said, bringing her gaze back to his. "That rug looks comfortable."

"I can't let you sleep on the floor," she replied, her voice slightly breathless. "We can share a bed without anything happening."

He gave her a long look. "I'm not so sure about that, Lexie."

Her stomach clenched at the gleam in his eyes. "To be honest, I'm not sure, either."

"Then I'll take the floor, as long as you share your pillows."

She stepped forward, putting her hands on his shoulders, feeling his muscles tighten beneath her touch. "Grayson..."

"What?" he asked, placing his hands on her hips. "Tell me what you want, Lexie."

It was suddenly all so simple. "I don't want you to sleep on the floor. I want you in the bed with me. I want to pick up where we left off earlier."

"Are you sure? I don't want this to happen just because there's one bed."

"That's not the reason. I want to be with you. I know that might not be the smartest idea, but I don't want to think about anything else right now. I just want us to be together," she said, looking into his eyes. When he didn't answer right away, she added, "And if you say no, you are definitely not getting a pillow."

He smiled at her nervous joke. "You think I'm going to say no? Do I look like I'm crazy?"

"Well, you haven't said yes."

"I wanted to be certain you didn't have anything else to say. I don't want you to feel pressured."

"I'm actually starting to feel like I'm pressuring you."

"You're not. But once I say yes, we are not going to be talking for a while, so if there's anything that needs to be said..."

His words sent a rush of desire through her. "I'm done talking. And I'm over having to stop kissing you when I really want to keep going—"

He cut off whatever else she might have had to say by crushing her mouth in a hot, feverish, demanding kiss that matched the need that had been building in her for weeks. She met his passion with her own, feeling dizzy with a hunger that seemed to grow with each kiss.

When they finally broke apart, he rested his forehead against hers.

"Lexie," he said, her name a whisper full of promise and longing.

"I know," she breathed. "I feel it too."

She began unbuttoning his shirt, her fingers trembling slightly.

He caught her hands, stilling them. "Are you really sure?"

"I've never been more certain of anything in my life."

He smiled and then picked her up, surprising her with the move. He carried her a few steps to the bed and gently put her down on the mattress, his eyes dark with desire and something deeper, something that created a lump in her throat because she'd never had anyone look at her the way he was looking at her, like he saw her, he really saw her, and he liked what he saw, not just her looks, but who she was on the inside.

"You're beautiful," he said, brushing a strand of hair from her face.

"I thought we weren't going to talk."

He smiled at that, slow and devastating, and leaned down to kiss her again, telling her without words exactly how he felt.

Lexie woke up Monday morning to the sound of Grayson's quiet breathing and the soft sunlight filtering through the cabin windows. For a moment, she lay perfectly still, savoring the weight of his arm around her waist, the way his dark hair fell across his forehead, the sexy morning stubble on his jaw, the peaceful expression that she'd never seen on his face when he was awake.

Their night together had been so much more than she'd imagined it could be. First times could be awkward, out of sync, but not with Grayson. Their bodies had moved together as if they'd been making love for years, as if they knew exactly what the other needed and when they needed it.

The man she knew to be driven, purposeful, and determined had brought all those traits to bed, loving her in a way she'd never been loved before, but he'd also been teasing and fun, and after they'd made love, they'd talked long into the night. She'd hated when sleep had finally caught up with her because she'd wanted to enjoy every minute, knowing they were on borrowed time.

But now the night was over, and she was a little sad about that, which made her realize there could be more hurt coming her way. It was the choice she'd made to have the night with Grayson, and she wouldn't regret it, no matter what came next.

Grayson suddenly shifted, his eyes flickering open, his lips parting with a smile when he saw her face.

"Good morning," he murmured, his voice rough with sleep.

"Good morning yourself," she said, turning in his arms to face him properly.

"How did you sleep?" he asked.

"Better than I have in weeks," she admitted. "But I was pretty tired by the time we finally fell asleep."

"You're not complaining, are you?"

"Not even a little bit," she said with a laugh.

"Good." He pulled her closer, pressing a soft kiss to her forehead. "Why don't I get dressed and check out what's for breakfast?"

"You don't have to wait on me," she protested.

"I want to. Besides, I'm fairly sure if I let you get dressed and start moving around, you'll remember you're a responsible adult with things to do."

"I think you're more likely to remember to be responsible than me," she said with a smile.

"Good point," he said, sitting up and reaching for his jeans. "But not today. I'm planning on a few more hours of irresponsible, if that's okay with you."

"More than okay." She watched him get dressed, admiring the play of morning light across his shoulders, the unselfconscious way he moved. When he leaned down to kiss her goodbye, she caught his face in her hands. "Grayson?"

"Yeah?"

"Last night was..." She struggled for words that wouldn't sound too heavy, too loaded with expectation.

"I know," he said softly. "For me too."

After he left, she wrapped herself in the inn's plush robe and stepped out onto the small porch. The desert morning was crisp and clear, the Joshua trees casting long shadows across the rocky landscape. This was exactly the kind of moment she'd usually be eager to capture, but she didn't want to be an observer today. She wanted to participate. She wanted to feel everything.

Ten minutes later, Grayson returned with a tray loaded with coffee, fresh blueberry muffins, and breakfast burritos.

They ate sitting cross-legged on the bed, sharing more stories about their lives. She told him about going to college at UCLA, law school at Georgetown, and then living with two wild party girls her first year working at her father's law firm. While they were hitting up the clubs, she was working until midnight as a first-year associate.

Grayson shared his experiences at Harvard and how his

freshman-year roommate almost got them both suspended for selling weed out of their room. He hadn't known anything about it but had no way to prove that. Fortunately, his roommate had come clean and admitted that Grayson knew nothing about his side hustle. The amount he was selling was very small, but because he was also failing his classes, his parents yanked him out of school until he could grow up and be worthy of their tuition money. "So, I ended up with my own room for the rest of the year," he finished.

"That turned out good for you."

"It did."

"One of my roommates met a guy who considered himself a health and wellness guru. He convinced her that material things were bad and that she should sell everything she had, and they could use the money to travel and see the world. She sold it all, and I should mention that her belongings had all been bought and paid for by her parents. They showed up a few days after she left. I thought she'd told them what she was doing, but she hadn't said a word. Suddenly, I had one less roommate sharing the rent and her hysterically crying mother asking me why I hadn't stopped her from leaving."

"I guess we both struck out in the roommate department."

"I have liked living alone the past two years."

"Are you really alone? You always seem to be surrounded by friends."

"Which is what's so great about Ocean Shores. My friends are there, but I still have my own space."

"The perfect solution," he said a little tightly.

She wiped her mouth with a napkin. "I brought up the forbidden subject, sorry."

"We can talk about whatever you want to talk about."

"Well, I don't want to talk about that. Not now. Not while we're having fun. I'm well aware there's an expiration date not too far in the future, but it's not today."

"No, it's not," he agreed.

She was about to say something when his phone buzzed. He pulled it out and read a text, his expression stiffening. "Work?" she asked.

"Yes. My Singapore deal is running into one obstacle after another."

"We can leave now if you want."

He hesitated, and she could see the battle going on in his eyes.

"Checkout isn't until eleven," he said, putting his phone on the nightstand. "We have a couple of hours."

"Really? I thought you were a man who always put work first."

"I thought I was, too. But when I'm around you, I'm different."

"Different good?"

"Different great."

She liked the way his eyes suddenly sparked. "What do you want to do with those hours?"

"I have a few ideas. None of them involves leaving this bed."

She picked up the tray of their empty dishes and put it on the dresser, then she got back onto the bed. "I'm in." She leaned over and kissed his lips, tasting coffee and possibilities. He pulled her against him, the robe sliding off her bare shoulders, and she stopped thinking about everything except him and the delicious way he whispered her name as his hands ran down her body.

They left their cozy cabin just after eleven, and Lexie was sorry to leave, but they couldn't put off the rest of their lives any longer. While conversation flowed easily for most of the trip, as they neared Ocean Shores, the easy intimacy of the morning began to splinter. The constant buzzing of Grayson's phone filled the silence between them, each vibration fraying the edges of the cozy cocoon they'd been living in.

"Someone is desperate to reach you," she said lightly.

He pulled into the parking lot at Ocean Shores and picked up his phone, his expression hardening as he took a quick look at the screen. "The Singapore deal is falling apart."

"What happened?"

"I took my eye off the ball. That's what happened."

She jerked at his tone. "It was your idea to stay in the cabin after you got the first call, not mine. I told you we could leave."

He dragged in a breath, regret filling his gaze. "I know. I'm sorry. It's just months of work falling apart. But those few hours aren't why this is happening."

"I understand. So, go fix it." She got out of the car, grabbed her camera bag from the back, and shut the door.

As she came around the car, he caught her arm in the parking lot, his gaze softer, almost pleading. "I didn't mean to ruin anything, Lexie. Yesterday, last night, this morning—it was good."

"It was," she agreed, happy with his words. She pressed a quick kiss to his lips. "The most fun I've had in a long time."

"I feel the same way, Lexie."

As their gazes clung together for far too long, she finally forced herself to pull away. "Good luck with your deal. I'll see you later."

She moved into the courtyard, pausing by the table where her aunt was working on a crossword puzzle while Grayson headed up the stairs to his apartment.

"You're back," Josie said, a curious gleam in her eyes. "I thought you were coming home last night."

"The highway was blocked by an accident. We had to find a motel."

"That sounds interesting."

She let out a sigh as she sat down at the table. "I feel guilty."

"Guilty? Why?"

"Because I deliberately tried to forget who Grayson is and how he holds our future in his hands. It was more fun to pretend the sale of this building wasn't an issue between us."

"You don't have to feel guilty for having fun, Lexie. Maybe your time together will help him change his mind."

"I don't know about that. He seems determined to keep business and personal separate. And to be honest, I was having such a good time with him that I didn't even try to talk to him about it. I feel like I let our community down."

"You didn't let anyone down, and you don't know what's going to happen." Josie gave her a sympathetic smile. "It's okay to like him, Lexie. As far as I know, he's a good man. He's intelligent and successful."

"He's all that and more. I just wish things were different," she said with a sigh.

"I still have hope it will all work out, but if it doesn't, then we'll do something else. We'll figure it out." She paused. "How was Joshua Tree?"

"The park was magnificent, the landscape mind-blowing. I hope my photographs match what I saw."

"I'm sure they do. I can't wait to see them."

"Is there anything else going on around here? Any sign of our mysterious tenant?"

"He's not mysterious; he's just private," Josie said with annoyance. "And as someone who ran from the media a long time ago, I know how important privacy can be."

"Does that mean he's famous? Is he an actor?"

Her aunt rolled her eyes and shook her head. "I am not telling you anything. When he's ready to tell his story, he will."

"Fine. Keep your secrets. I'm too tired to be nosy."

"Maybe you should tell me why you're so tired," Josie said with a laugh.

"I'm not ready to tell that story," she said, smiling back at her aunt as she got up from the table.

"I didn't think you were."

After leaving her aunt, she walked into her apartment and set down her things. There was a lot she could do, but she felt suddenly exhausted and emotionally drained. She also couldn't stop thinking about what Grayson was dealing with.

On impulse, she picked up her phone and sent him a text. Maybe he wouldn't appreciate her concern, but she still wanted to say something. *Hope it all works out in Singapore*, she texted. *Thanks again for going with me. I had a great time.*

He didn't reply, and she stared at the phone for far too long. She told herself he was just dealing with his crisis. And whether he responded or not, at least he would know she cared, and maybe that's all that mattered.

She went into her bedroom and changed into some comfy shorts and a tank top, then curled up on her bed with her phone. She looked through some social media sites and impulsively typed in Jax Ridley's name, but nothing came up, at least not for anyone famous. Maybe his name wasn't really Jax Ridley. On the other hand, that was an unusual name. It didn't sound like an alias, and she remembered seeing it on his check on Josie's counter. But maybe his real name wasn't his famous name...

She smiled to herself, knowing she was making up a story that probably wasn't anywhere close to the truth, but it was a distraction. Then a text flashed on her phone, and her pulse jumped. It was from Grayson: *I'm trying to salvage the deal, but I'm not sure that's possible. I may be out of touch for a while.*

She was glad he'd answered, but she wished she could do more: *I can't help you with your deal, but I'd be happy to bring you dinner later.*

Thanks for the offer, but I need to focus on this. I'll talk to you soon.

There was really nothing she could say to that except: *Good luck.*

He texted her a thumbs-up, which was the least romantic emoji she could have gotten. She had a feeling the romance was probably over, even though it had barely gotten started. But

Grayson's failing deal had just reminded him that this trip to Ocean Shores was a waste of his time. He'd basically said that when he'd first gotten the news. While he'd apologized immediately, saying he didn't mean it like that, she had a feeling that's exactly what he'd meant.

CHAPTER SIXTEEN

Grayson had said he would talk to her soon. That had been on Monday afternoon. It was now Thursday evening, and Lexie hadn't heard a word from him. Nor had she seen him around the building, although she had seen the light on in his apartment late into the night. Clearly, he was consumed with work. She'd thought about checking in a million times, but he hadn't been open to her help the last time she'd asked, even if it was just bringing him food. She needed to let him be. She just didn't really want to.

After finishing up her shoot at an anniversary party, she stepped into the courtyard just after seven and spotted Kaia sharing a pizza with Ben and Serena. Baby Amanda snoozed nearby in her stroller.

"Well, look who's here," Kaia said. "My long-lost friend, who has had no time to chat since her trip to Joshua Tree."

"Sorry, I've been busy," she said.

"Well, you're not busy now, so sit down. We have plenty of pizza if you're hungry."

"I already ate." She leaned over the stroller. "Amanda is an angel."

"Only when she's asleep," Serena muttered, dark circles

under her eyes. "The rest of the time she screams like she's auditioning for the opera."

She smiled. "If you ever need a break, I'd be happy to babysit."

"Don't joke," Serena warned. "I'll take you up on it."

"I mean it. I babysat a lot growing up. I'm pretty good with kids."

Serena's eyes softened as she gazed at her daughter. "Maybe in a week or so. We're still figuring out breastfeeding and pumping."

"Okay, that's my cue to go," Ben said dryly, pushing back his chair.

"Sorry, no more breast-pump talk," Serena promised.

"It's fine. I have to work tonight."

As he left, Amanda stirred, and Serena groaned. "Time to feed this angel. See you later." She wheeled the stroller away, leaving Lexie and Kaia alone.

"And then there were two," Kaia said with a laugh. "Now you can tell me what happened with you and Grayson last weekend. Did you spend the night with him in Joshua Tree?"

"Yes, and I think it was a big mistake."

"Because it was bad?"

"Because it was great." She blew out a sigh of frustration. "I don't regret it, but now I feel strange about it because I haven't talked to Grayson since we got back. I know he's tied up on a business deal, but it feels like he's using that to push me away."

Kaia's gaze filled with sympathy. "I'm sorry, Lex."

"We had so much fun, Kaia, the best time I've had in forever. We got along so well. We talked and talked and..."

"And..." Kaia prodded. "While I'm interested in the talking, I'm far more curious about the rest of that sentence."

"The rest of it was great, too." Her cheeks warmed at the memories. "The freeway was closed, and we had to spend the night somewhere. There weren't any choices except this cute bed-and-breakfast with rustic cottages, and they only had one left. We had to take it."

"Of course you did," Kaia said with a smile. "And I'm not judging. You could do a lot worse than an attractive billionaire."

"I'm not sure he's a billionaire, but he is very attractive," she said, feeling an ache in her gut. "It's hard to meet someone you really feel connected to, like you can totally be yourself, and they can be themselves."

"I'll say it is."

"I just wish he wasn't our landlord. If he sells the building, I'll not only lose my home, but I'll never see him again."

"Did he say he was going to sell?"

"We didn't talk about it. But he's been honest about his intentions since the beginning."

"Well, he's going to do what he's going to do."

"You sound like Josie. When did everyone get to be so fatalistic?" she complained.

"When we realized there was nothing we could do," Kaia answered. "You've fought hard to make him see that this is more than just a building, Lexie. And obviously, he likes you. If you can't convince him not to sell, there's nothing I can do, nothing anyone can do."

"I should have used the time I had to pressure him into keeping the building intact. But I didn't do that. I got lost in the moment, and that was a mistake. I'm sorry."

"Oh, my God! Stop apologizing! Saving this building isn't on you, and no one is going to hold it against you if Grayson decides to sell."

"I'll hold it against me."

"Well, you're going to have to figure out how not to do that. Anyway, we still have time. Frank told me that Grayson is going to help him with the car tomorrow to get it ready for the car show on Saturday."

"Well, that's good. Maybe he's resolved his business problems if he has time to work on the car." She was both happy and annoyed that he'd had time to talk to Frank but not to her. Maybe he did have regrets about what had happened between them. "Let's change the subject," she said, looking back at Kaia. "How's your doctor?"

"Not happening," Kaia said shortly.

She was surprised. "Why? I thought you had a good first date."

"First date was good. Second date was better. Third date became a disaster when his alleged ex-girlfriend showed up right when we were about to have sex."

"Why do you say alleged?"

"Because seeing the way he reacted to her unhappiness was very illuminating. He's not over her. I don't care what he says. I saw the way he looked at her. And, apparently, she was the one who broke it off and is now having second thoughts. I think he wants her back, and I don't need to be in the middle of that drama."

"That's too bad. I was hoping for good things."

She shrugged. "Me, too. But it's fine." She picked up the bottle of wine on the table and an empty glass. "Ben didn't want any wine since he's working tonight, but maybe you do?"

"I do," she admitted. "Have I missed any other gossip the last few days?"

Kaia poured her some wine, then handed her the glass. "Paige went on a date with a divorced dad, who has a kid a few years older than Henry. She's guardedly optimistic. But you know what's interesting is that Ben didn't look at all happy about it when she was telling me. I think he has a crush on her."

"Really? I've never noticed any flirting between them."

"Well, my brother is a horrible flirt, so that's not surprising. Maybe it's nothing. Maybe I just want someone in my family to find love. My father complained to me about his lack of grandchildren the other day. Not that he would say that to either of my brothers, but for me to be in my thirties now and single seems to be appalling to him. And this was the man who raised me to be a tomboy. I don't know why he would think I would spend all my time looking for a husband."

She smiled at Kaia's rant. "See, this is why it's good my parents don't talk to me anymore; I don't have to hear their criticism or their concern about my judgment or my singleness."

"We should drink to us," Kaia said, raising her glass. "Because we're awesome on our own."

She clinked her glass against Kaia's. "Speaking of being awesome, the photos I took at the caves and at Joshua Tree are really good. I spoke to Sienna at the gallery today, and my show is set for the Fourth of July weekend. I'll still need to add to my collection, but I feel more confident now."

"That's great. I love seeing your new energy and excitement. It's felt like you've been stuck in a rut the last several months."

"A rut of my own making. But I'm getting out of it." She paused as she saw Grayson coming down the stairs wearing running pants and a T-shirt. He hesitated for a second when he saw them, but then he walked over to their table.

"Hello, ladies," he said smoothly. "What are you up to?"

Lexie forced brightness into her voice. "I just got back from photographing an anniversary party and crashed Kaia's pizza party."

"Which wasn't a party," Kaia said. "Just a few friends having dinner. Are you off for a run?"

"Yes. I need to burn off a day chained to my computer."

"How's the deal going?" she asked.

"Still up in the air." His jaw tightened. "I'm trying to find new angles."

She saw the shadows under his eyes, the strain pulling at him. She wanted to reach out, to ask more questions, to make him let her in. And for one long moment, his gaze held hers. The air between them buzzed, an echo of everything they hadn't said.

Then he straightened, voice cool again. "I should go. Still more work to do tonight. I'll see you both later."

She felt the sting of the plural. See you *both*. Not her. Them. "Well, that's done," she said heavily.

"No way," Kaia said, shaking her head in disagreement. "The way you and Grayson looked at each other gave me goose bumps. I felt like I was watching a movie between two star-crossed lovers. I don't know what's going to happen between you two, Lexie, but I know one thing for sure: it is not over, not by a long shot."

She really wanted Kaia to be right.

Grayson headed out of his apartment Friday afternoon, desperately needing the month at Ocean Shores to be over, but he still had a week to go. Even with his problems on the Singapore project and his need to be back in his office with the rest of the team, his father was refusing to budge on the agreement they'd made. So, he was stuck here, and he didn't know what to do about it.

Nothing was going the way he wanted it to go. His deal was floundering. His relationship with Lexie was not in a good place. Their one short encounter after their Joshua Tree trip had been agonizingly uncomfortable, which was completely his fault. He was sending her mixed signals, but he didn't know what to do about that.

They'd gotten very close on their trip. But their escape from reality was always going to be temporary. It had just ended sooner than he would have liked.

When the Singapore acquisition had fallen apart, he'd had to focus solely on getting it back. It was what he'd been working on for months. It was how he was going to prove to his father that the company would not only be in good hands but in better hands when he took over. Now, he didn't know if that would happen. But he'd done all he could do for now. He'd sent over new contracts. He'd had a dozen conversations with a dozen different people, and they'd regroup on Monday.

With time on his hands, he'd decided to help Frank put the finishing touches on the Mustang. The car show was tomorrow, and Frank was determined to drive the car in the parade. He felt bad that he'd dropped the ball on this project, but Frank had been understanding, just saying he knew he was busy, but if he had time…

Well, he finally had time. When he got to the parking lot, he was impressed with all that Frank had accomplished. The car looked good, with fresh red paint sparkling in the late afternoon light, the chrome bumpers polished, and new tires mounted and balanced.

Frank wiped his hands on a shop rag as he leaned over the engine bay, making final adjustments to the carburetor.

"There you are," Frank said, looking up with a smile as Grayson approached. "Hand me that timing light," he added, gesturing toward the workbench.

He handed him the tool. "You've made incredible progress."

"Thanks. I'm almost there," he said as he connected the timing light to the spark plug wire. "Fire her up."

Grayson slid behind the wheel and turned the key. The engine roared to life with a deep, throaty rumble, then Frank made a subtle adjustment, and the idle smoothed out into a perfect, powerful purr.

"That's it," Frank called over the engine noise. "Shut her down."

He slid out of the car as Frank continued to tinker under the hood. "She sounds good to me."

"Yeah, I'm just double-checking everything. I could use your sharp eye to make sure I haven't missed anything. Once we've checked all the boxes, tomorrow, I'll give her one final wash and detail. She's going to turn heads at that show."

"She will," he agreed.

Frank met his gaze. "I'd like you to ride with me in the parade. What do you say?"

"This is your victory lap, not mine."

"You helped me more than you know."

"I've been MIA the past three weeks."

"Yeah, but when you first helped me, I was having doubts about whether I could even restore this car or not, and your encouragement made me believe I could. So, will you ride with me?"

"I'd be honored," he said, touched by Frank's words. "What can I do to help you now?"

"Before we get into that," Frank said, giving him a speculative look. "Why don't you tell me what's been keeping you so busy?"

"I've been working on an acquisition of a property in Singapore for months, and it's falling apart at the eleventh hour."

"That's a shame."

"Yeah." He ran a hand through his hair in weariness and frustration. "Six months of due diligence, negotiations, flying back and forth to meetings. And now everything's going sideways. The seller's debt is worse than they disclosed, there are environmental issues with the building, and the asking price just doubled because another buyer entered the picture."

Frank leaned against the car, giving him his full attention. "What does your gut tell you?"

"That's just it—I don't know anymore."

"Yes, you do. I worked with a lot of executives in my forty years as a corporate attorney, and I've seen men and women who do their research, investigate every alternative until they're sure they know exactly what they're doing. I've also seen execs who have absolutely no substance, but they can hype, spin, and pretend like nobody's business. They think short term, not long term. They want to win now, especially if it looks like a win. They tell themselves they'll fix the other problems later or maybe not at all if nothing comes back to bite them in the ass."

"I know that type," he admitted.

"I would venture to say you fall into the first category. Because I've seen you work on this car, and you don't go too fast, you don't cut corners."

"That's true."

"Your instincts are sound, Grayson. What are they telling you? Should you keep throwing money and time at this project, telling yourself you've already invested too much to quit, or do you let it go? Do you ask yourself if you were starting fresh today, knowing what you know now, would you still want to develop this property."

He stared back at Frank, his words resonating. "That's a good question."

"See, the hard truth is," Frank continued, "your ideal plan—the one you fell in love with at the beginning—that's already gone. What you're looking at now is a completely different animal. The real decision isn't about whether you can salvage what you originally wanted. It's whether this new version—this battered, expensive, problematic version—is something you'd choose to take on from scratch."

"I'd be walking away from months of work. I'd have nothing to show for my time," he argued. "I can't quit."

"Then you'll have to keep plugging holes in a sinking ship. Maybe you stop the ship from going under, but will that ship be something you're proud of?" Frank picked up a rag and began wiping down his hands. "There's a difference between persistence and stubbornness. Persistence is when you keep working toward your goal despite obstacles. Stubbornness is when you keep working toward a goal that no longer exists."

He smiled. "That might be the best advice anyone has ever given me."

"Well, most people don't take my advice," Frank said with a laugh. "But you have it, for what's worth. Now, are you ready to get your hands dirty?"

Before he could answer, his gaze caught on Lexie walking through the parking lot, and his body tightened at the sight of her. She wore a simple white T-shirt knotted at her waist and denim shorts with frayed hems that showed off her tanned legs. She had a leather portfolio tucked under her arm.

"How's it going?" she asked, pausing a few feet away, her eyes moving between the two men.

"We just finished the final engine adjustments," Frank said.

As Frank added other details to expand on his answer, he found himself staring at Lexie. He couldn't hear what Frank was saying because his heart was pounding in his head. She was so damn beautiful. What the hell was he doing staying away from her?

Lexie's attention was wavering the longer Frank's answer went on, her gaze darting to his, and there was something electric in the air between them as they had an unspoken conversation.

He wanted to walk over to her, pull her close, and kiss her sweet, sexy mouth.

But he couldn't. Not with Frank watching, not with everything so complicated between them.

"Lexie?" Frank's voice turned sharper, breaking their connection.

"Yes?" she asked a little breathlessly.

"Are you coming to the car show tomorrow?" Frank asked, seemingly oblivious to the tension crackling between his two companions.

"Wouldn't miss it," Lexie replied, though her eyes never left Grayson's face. "I love seeing all the restored classics."

"Good. Grayson is going to ride with me in the parade."

She smiled. "That should be fun. I'll be sure to get a photo of that."

"Speaking of photos," he said, tipping his head toward her portfolio. "Are those the photographs you took at Joshua Tree?"

"It's a small selection of photos from the caves and Joshua Tree. I wanted to show the gallery what I'm working on."

"Can I see?" he asked, feeling a desperate need to keep her close.

"Sure."

She pulled out several prints, and both he and Frank stepped closer to take a look.

The first photo captured the twisted Joshua trees, the otherworldly rock formations, and the dramatic desert light. The second photo was from the caves—not the one of him, but another of a gold chain hanging from a dark, rocky crevice, the contrast between the sparkle and the edgy darkness creating a story that everyone would want an answer to. And the third photo was the most surprising.

It had been taken at the lodge he'd gone to investigate, the one with the faded neon sign, the cracked stucco and drained pool, the weed-filled former garden. She'd captured something haunting and beautiful in its decay, with desert wildflowers growing through cracks in the concrete. It was a place that could be brought back to life, full of possibility rather than just deterioration.

"Wow," he said quietly. "These are incredible." He wasn't just seeing the photos; he was seeing her in the images, her creativity, her unique way of looking at life.

"I agree," Frank said as she put the prints away. "I had no idea you were so talented, Lexie."

"Thanks, Frank. I'm excited about the direction my collection is taking. I'm starting to think maybe these photos are good enough to display."

"They're better than good," he told her. "They all tell a story."

"I think so, too," she said with excitement. "As I was selecting the photos, the ones that resonated the most were the ones that came with a question, like where is this place, why is that gold chain stuck in a cave, and who lost it there? Anyway, I'm getting carried away," she said. "I know they're just pictures."

"They're art," Frank said. "And you're allowed to be excited."

"Thanks. I better go. I have my day job to get to."

"What is it today?" he asked.

"I'm doing headshots for a corporation downtown. It will not be anywhere near as creative as this. But there will still be the challenge to make everyone look good, so I'm going to focus on how every job makes me better, no matter what it is."

"That's a good attitude."

"Dare I ask about your deal, Grayson?"

"It's still teetering on the edge of collapse, but I won't know anything more until Monday. So, I'm going to help Frank get this baby ready to roll."

"I'll let you get back to it."

He watched her walk into the building, and when he turned back to Frank, he saw a knowing gleam in the man's eyes.

"That girl is something special," Frank said.

"I can't disagree," he murmured, thinking about how her creative passion inspired him, how her laugh made something in his chest feel lighter. How talking to her made him feel alive. How making love to her had taken every sense to a new height. How impossible it was going to be to say goodbye to her when this was all over.

CHAPTER SEVENTEEN

Lexie positioned herself near the end of the parade route, her camera ready as the procession of classic cars made their way down Ocean Boulevard. The noon sun was brilliant overhead, and she could hear the rumble of engines long before she could see the cars themselves. She was joined by Josie and Margaret, who were very close to Frank, as well as Kaia, who'd grumbled that she had nothing better to do, and her brother, Ben, who was apparently also a fan of old cars.

"There!" Josie pointed excitedly as Frank's restored Mustang came into view. "The car looks so good!"

"I never would have imagined that piece of old junk that I saw a month ago could look that good," Margaret agreed.

Lexie raised her camera and snapped several shots as the Mustang rolled past. Frank was grinning behind the wheel, clearly in his element. Grayson sat in the passenger seat looking handsome and relaxed, happy to be cruising Ocean Boulevard in a Mustang with a man old enough to be his father.

As the car passed their group, his gaze met hers, and she felt the familiar flutter in her chest that she'd been trying to ignore all week.

"That car is a work of art," Ben said. "I helped Frank source some of the original parts months ago, but I wasn't sure he could pull this off."

"I didn't know you were also a vintage car enthusiast, Ben," she said.

"My brother and I had to put our first car together with parts we found at a junkyard." Ben's expression grew wistful. "Some of my best memories."

"And some of my worst memories," Kaia cut in. "You two would never let me help, and every time Dad came home and saw what you'd done, he'd brag about you for hours. It was so annoying."

Ben laughed. "You didn't want to help. You had no interest in that car."

"True. But I didn't like the attention you got from Dad." Kaia turned to her. "Ben and my brother were always my father's favorites."

"Not so," Ben said. "Dad had a soft spot for you, and you could weasel your way out of punishment with just a smile." He pointed to an old Thunderbird now crossing in front of them. "Look at that beauty."

Both she and Kaia dutifully obeyed, but now that the Mustang was turning into the field that had been transformed into a parking lot for the show, she had lost interest in the parade. "Let's check out the cars up close."

"Good idea," Ben said.

Josie and Margaret followed behind them as they walked two blocks to the field where rows of vehicles were lined up, their hoods popped open to display pristine engines. Food trucks lined the perimeter—a taco stand, a gourmet grilled cheese booth, and an ice cream truck with hand-painted signs advertising homemade waffle cones. A DJ played hits from the seventies and eighties, and families spread blankets on the grass while kids ran between the cars and the food trucks with wide-eyed enthusiasm.

They caught up with Grayson and Frank, who were talking to

a group of five or six men. Frank was in his element, answering questions about the restoration process. Grayson seemed content to chat with the other men gathered around the car.

As Josie and Margaret headed off to get drinks, she shot photos while Kaia looked at her phone and Ben wandered down the line of cars.

"This is boring," Kaia said a moment later.

"I think it's fun to see all these old cars restored."

"Really?" she asked doubtfully.

"Kaia," Ben called out as he moved quickly back to them. "Come with me. I want you to meet a friend of mine."

Kaia groaned dramatically. "If this is another one of your cop buddies who thinks talking about horsepower counts as flirting—"

"Hey, at least my friends aren't stalkers and don't have ex-girlfriends showing up at their doors in tears," Ben shot back. "Your track record isn't exactly stellar, sis."

"Okay, fine, I haven't been lucky in the dating department," Kaia admitted. "But that doesn't mean I need you playing matchmaker."

"I'm not setting you up, just asking you to say hello. There he is." Ben tipped his head toward the tall, dark-haired man coming around the back of a '67 Corvette.

Lexie watched Kaia's expression transform from boredom to interest.

"Seriously?" Kaia asked. "Maybe I underestimated you, Ben."

"You always do," he said.

Lexie smiled to herself as Ben walked Kaia over to his friend.

Since the last thing she wanted was for Grayson to see her standing alone, watching him like some lovesick teenager, she decided to get some ice cream.

The ice cream truck had a decent line, mostly families with children debating between rocket pops and ice cream sandwiches. While she was waiting, she checked her phone for any emails, but thankfully, all was quiet on the work front. As someone slid into line behind her, she lifted her head, her heart jumping into her throat when she realized it was Grayson.

"Good day for ice cream," he said.

"It is. I'm surprised you didn't wait for me to leave, though. You've been avoiding me as much as possible."

"Didn't we just chat yesterday when you showed me your photos?"

"Because you were with Frank, and I had to walk by you to go into the complex," she said dryly. "Otherwise, you've been avoiding me."

"It's been a busy week."

"Don't." She held up a hand. "It wasn't just work, and you know it. You backed off after our night in Joshua Tree. I know you had business to deal with, but I think you used that as an excuse not to see me."

For a moment, she thought he might deny it. Then he tipped his head in agreement. "You're right. Part of it was work, but part of it..." He ran a hand through his hair. "I don't know how to juggle everything and everyone."

"This isn't really about juggling, is it?" She stepped forward as the line moved. "It's not about finding time," she added. "It's about whether you want to make time. And you have to decide if that's what you want to do—or not."

He didn't answer, and the line shifted again, placing her at the order window. "I'll take a mint chip," she said.

"Rocky road for me." Grayson put a hand on her shoulder as he slid a ten-dollar bill across the counter.

She didn't bother to complain since he could certainly afford to buy her ice cream. A moment later, with their cones in hand, they stepped away from the truck.

"So, rocky road," she said as he licked his cone. "Seems like an appropriate choice."

He grinned. "I didn't realize that until I said it, but it was the perfect choice." He paused. "I heard what you said, Lexie. And you're not completely wrong. But it's not as simple as wanting to make time."

"I think it is."

He was quiet for a moment, studying her face, as they both ate their ice cream. Then, he said, "Let me ask you something. What do you want from this? From us?"

The question caught her off guard with its directness. "I don't know," she admitted.

"So you want me to know when you don't know yourself?" he challenged.

She felt heat rise in her cheeks. "That's not fair. I haven't been avoiding you. I wanted to spend time with you to see where things could go. But clearly you did not. Which is why we don't even need to have this conversation. You know what you want; you just don't want to say it. But I'd rather have someone tell me the truth than ghost me."

"I wasn't trying to ghost you. It's just complicated."

"I am very aware of how complicated it is. We have a huge conflict of interest. But this isn't about the building, it's about us."

He gave her a long, serious look, then said, "I do care about you, Lexie. I'm just afraid we can't both get what we want. That we're headed for disaster."

"We've been heading toward that cliff this whole time, and it hasn't stopped either one of us, because we have an undeniable connection."

"We do, but the edge of the cliff is getting closer."

"I know. Our time is running out. But the worst part of this past week hasn't been wondering what you're going to decide about Ocean Shores; it's been not being able to talk to you at all."

"How can we talk when we're on opposite sides?" His voice carried a note of frustration.

"I don't know, but I think we should."

He was about to say something when his phone buzzed. He

pulled it out, frowning at the screen. "This is about work. I didn't think I would hear anything until Monday. I'm sorry, I need to make a call." He paused. "I do want to talk to you, Lexie. I just can't do it now."

"I understand. Go. I'm going to catch up with my friends."

She watched him walk a few steps away and make a call, his free hand already running through his hair in that gesture she'd come to recognize as his stress tell. She could see him nod, his posture stiffening with each word he was hearing.

She stood there with her melting ice cream cone, watching the man she was falling for disappear back into his other world, and wondered if he would actually come back to finish their conversation, or if this was just how it would always be between them.

Maybe it was better if she didn't wait around to find out.

Since Kaia and Ben were talking to Ben's friend, and her aunt and Margaret were with Frank, Lexie decided to head home. She didn't know what was going on with Grayson, but she knew that she couldn't keep waiting for him. In fact, as she walked home, she realized that was the first time she'd admitted to herself that she was waiting. And she didn't like it.

She might have to wait for his decision on the sale of the building. But she didn't have to wait to hear whether or not he wanted to have a relationship with her. She had her own work to do, and she had never waited to make her own plans because of a guy. She'd learned that was a bad idea when she was sixteen years old and she had waited until eight o'clock on a Saturday night for Christian Parker to ask her to meet him at a party. But he didn't call, and she didn't go anywhere. Later, she'd found out he was making out with someone else at the party he hadn't invited her to. She'd vowed then and there she would never wait again, and she'd mostly kept that promise to herself.

But now, she was doing that with Grayson, and it was time to stop.

By the time she got back to her apartment, she'd worked up a lot of angry energy, and when she walked into her dining room and looked at her wall of inspiration, she realized just how long she'd been putting off her real career. She ripped down the inspiration photos one by one. It felt oddly satisfying to erase her wall of insecurity. She didn't need the work of others to inspire her; she needed to inspire herself.

Once all the old photos were down, she started taping some of her extra prints up. She'd made two copies of the photos she would use in the show, and as she created her own wall of inspiration, she started to realize just how good she was.

There were still blank spaces, but what she had now was so much better than what she'd had on the wall before, because it was her work, and she was proud of what she'd done so far. But this was only the beginning.

Her phone rang, and she jumped. She'd been so caught up in what she was doing, she'd lost track of time and everything else. It was Sienna from the Art Nest.

"I'm so glad I caught you, Lexie," Sienna said. "I have an interesting offer for you. A friend of mine works for *New Frontiers* magazine. She buys photos from freelancers, and I showed her the digital copies that you sent me for your show, and she would love to acquire the photos you took at Joshua Tree."

"Really? That's amazing."

"There's more. She had a commissioned shoot set up in Morocco, but her photographer bailed, and she needs a replacement fast. She can pay airfare and hotel for a five-day trip, plus whatever you negotiate for the photos. But the shoot is in a week. You would have to commit soon, like today or tomorrow, or else she'll keep looking."

"Wow. That's a lot to take in. Did you say Morocco?" she asked.

"Yes. I think you should do it, Lexie. You're so good. And whatever photos you don't sell to her will probably work great in your collection. This could be a great way to get into the magazine as well. They don't hire staffers, but if you can become one of their preferred freelancers, you can sometimes get commissions, like this one. Plus, you'll have time to shoot other things while you're there."

"My head is spinning."

"I know," Sienna said with an understanding laugh. "She wanted to call you directly, but I thought it would be better if I warmed you up first. I gave her your number, and if you're interested, she'll call you at five today. Just say the word."

"Yes. I'm definitely interested."

"Then I'll have her call you at five, and you two figure out the rest. Good luck, Lexie."

"Thanks again, Sienna. This is amazing."

"I'm happy to help someone as talented as you."

As she set down the phone, she let out a breath, still amazed by the opportunity that had just landed in her lap. She couldn't believe what was happening. A job in Morocco? How could she turn that down? She opened her calendar app. She didn't have any weddings scheduled for the next two weeks, which was good, because those contracts were impossible to break. Her other jobs could probably be rearranged or postponed.

A knock came at her door, and she wondered if the day was going to get even better if Grayson had decided to stop avoiding her. But it wasn't Grayson; it was her aunt.

"Aunt Josie," she said with a short smile. "Come in."

"I'm guessing I'm not the one you were hoping to see," Josie said with a knowing gleam in her eyes.

"I wasn't hoping to see anyone," she lied.

"I brought you the book I was telling you about." She held it up in her hand. "I finally finished it, and I think you'll love it."

She took the book as her aunt stepped into the apartment

and shut the door behind her. "Thank you, but I don't think I'll have time for reading for a while."

As she set the book down on her dining room table, her aunt said, "Well, this is different. You changed the wall to your photographs."

"I thought it was time to look to myself for inspiration, instead of someone else."

"Good for you." Josie moved closer to the wall. "These are gorgeous. They'll sell in an instant when they go up in the gallery. Sienna is going to be delighted with all of this and more. I'm sure you're not done yet."

"I'm not done. I just got a crazy good invitation from Sienna. Her friend who works for *New Frontiers* magazine wants to buy my Joshua Tree photos, and she's also interested in hiring me for a shoot in Morocco."

"What? That is wonderful."

"The woman is going to call me at five today with the details, but I'd have to leave in about a week." She looked at her watch. "I have two hours to figure out how I can manage that."

"What's to figure out? You'll go to Morocco, shoot photos, and have the time of your life."

"But I have responsibilities. I have jobs I'll have to reschedule. Some of those clients might get angry. And I won't be able to help you as much."

"I can get by without your help, not that I don't appreciate it. But I would never stand in the way of you doing what you were meant to do."

"Maybe I'm not good enough." The words flew out of her mouth before she could stop them.

Josie gave her a firm look. "Not a chance. Look at the wall, Lexie."

Her gaze flickered to the wall, then back to her aunt. "You're right. I'm just scared, but I'm also excited. I haven't traveled much and certainly not to a place like Morocco."

"This could be the beginning of a new chapter in your life."

"I'm just not sure I'm done with this chapter. I could be gone when Grayson makes his decision. If the building is going to be sold, there will be a lot to do in a short time. How can I not be here to help you through that?"

"If Grayson decides to sell, we'll have time to get organized and figure out our next move. I don't want you to make decisions based on that, because we don't know what's going to happen."

Despite her aunt's words, she didn't seem as unconcerned as she'd once been. "Do you know something?" she asked. "Because you're the one who has had faith this is all going to work out since the beginning. Now, you don't seem as certain."

"I still have hope that it will," Josie said. "But I did see Grayson put a suitcase into his car a short while ago before he drove away. Maybe it's just a short business trip, and he'll be back."

"Or maybe he's never coming back," she said heavily.

"Oh, honey, don't look so sad. We'll survive whatever is coming."

"I know we will. I just wish things were different. I wish Grayson wasn't hell-bent on selling our home. I thought once he was here, he would see how great it is."

"And you thought he would see how great you are, and he wouldn't be able to hurt you."

"Maybe," she conceded. "I know he doesn't want to hurt me. He's just very determined to make money for his father's business so that when he takes over officially, his father will believe it's in good hands. I'm also aware that this building sits on very valuable land. I'm sure he could make a fortune by selling it. I just don't want him to take away the place that I love."

"I understand. And you're not just unhappy about the possibility of losing this building; you're sad about Grayson. You're in love with him."

"No. It's not love. It's not that serious."

"Is that true or just what you're telling yourself?"

"Maybe a little of both," she admitted. "But whatever it is, I'll get over it, right?"

"Perhaps in Morocco," her aunt suggested.

She gave her a somewhat sad smile. "Perhaps so."

CHAPTER EIGHTEEN

Grayson walked into his father's office on Monday morning. He'd spent Saturday night and Sunday in his LA apartment trying to salvage his deal and also remember who he was and what he wanted, because after three weeks in Ocean Shores and his whirlwind relationship with Lexie, he wasn't sure if he'd really changed or if he'd just gotten caught up in a moment.

By the time Monday morning rolled around, he was only sure of one thing, and that was that he needed to speak to his father.

Emerson Holt's corner office overlooked downtown Los Angeles from a commanding view on the thirty-second floor of the Cromwell Building. It was the kind of space meant to inspire those who stepped into the office suite. It was also the kind of space he had always aspired to inherit, and that day was coming soon, but standing here now, he didn't feel the same sense of anticipation he once had. Instead, he was filled with a restless energy.

His father leaned back in his chair, giving him a thoughtful look. "What are you doing here, Grayson? You still have a week left at Ocean Shores."

"The Singapore deal isn't going to happen," he said, taking a seat in the leather chair facing his father's massive desk.

"I had a feeling. It's disappointing but not catastrophic. We can recover from this."

"Not without taking a loss."

"It not the first; it won't be the last. I'm actually impressed you decided to pull the plug."

His father's words reminded him of what Frank had said. "Well, I don't want to spend the next few years trying to plug up the leaky holes in that sinking ship."

"Sometimes, you have to cut your losses," Emerson agreed. "But I know you're disappointed. Your vision for the property was excellent. Hopefully, you can find something similar somewhere else to develop. But we could have had this conversation on the phone. I already read the report you sent last night to the executive team. Why are you here and not where I asked you to be?"

"I can't stay there anymore. You have to let me out of the agreement."

"Why? And don't give me some bullshit reason about how Singapore is an example of why you shouldn't be working from Ocean Shores, because your location didn't affect this at all."

"I'm not sure that's true. I took my eye off the ball. I was distracted. I wasn't working ten hours a day. I was fixing up an old car and exploring caves and a park with crazy ass trees in it."

His father smiled. "I have no idea what you're talking about, but it doesn't sound like you've been having a horrible time. Tell me about the cave. Is it where you can only get in during certain tidal patterns?"

"That's exactly how it works. How did you know that? And don't you give me some bullshit answer about how you read about the cave. You spent time at Ocean Shores, didn't you? You were in that cave."

"I was," his father admitted. "Thirty-five years ago, six months before I married your mother."

"And that's when you bought the Ocean Shores property. Why didn't you tell me you'd been there?"

He shrugged. "I had my reasons."

"What reasons? It's time to stop being so mysterious and tell me why the hell you sent me there."

"I wanted you to experience a different way of life."

"What does that mean?"

"The last few years, I've been very proud of the man you've become, Grayson. I've been honored to work alongside you, impressed with your intelligence, your business savvy..."

"You taught me everything I know."

"But I didn't teach you how to have a balanced life. I didn't teach you about prioritizing your happiness over your work."

"Why can't they be the same thing? They were for you. Right?"

"Most of the time. Actually, no. Not most of the time." He paused. "Thirty-five years ago, I attended a business conference in San Diego. After it ended, I decided to take two weeks off work. I was feeling so stressed and pressured, I was actually having heart palpitations. It was all too much, and I had to take a break." He took a breath. "It wasn't just work that was making me tense; it was also your mother. We'd been dating for a year, and she wanted to get married. She wanted to merge her father's company with mine. She thought we could be a power couple, and I thought so, too. But I wasn't sure I was ready to get married."

"Why didn't you just tell her that?"

"Oh, I did. And she always said there was no rush, but her words and actions didn't match. And her father's company was a tantalizing offer. He wanted me to be the son he'd never had. He wanted to give me a chance to really grow my business that I had spent ten years of insanely long hours working on."

"You're making your relationship sound like a business deal," he said with a frown.

"I didn't mean it like that," his father said. "I really cared about your mother. But she was as driven as I was. She wanted a lifestyle like the one she'd grown up in. She wanted a man like her father." He paused. "It's hard to explain, but I felt conflicted about everything. And then I met this woman on the beach, this free-spirited, red-haired, quirky woman who had a smile as bright as the sun and an energy for life that felt unmatched. We started spending time together. I came to find out she had left a bad marriage, a poor work environment, and was starting all over. She seemed so brave to me, so determined to live life on her terms, and I was captivated."

"Was her name Josie?" he asked, confident he already knew the answer.

"Yes. And she lived in this apartment building by the beach. My two-week vacation lasted four weeks. We had a passionate love affair. It was wrong. I knew it, and I couldn't stop myself. When I was with her, I felt more like myself than I had in years. But I knew it wasn't my real life. I had a business to get back to. Your mother was calling me all the time. I felt guilty and horrible about it all."

"So you ended it?"

"Josie ended it right after I told her I loved her. She said I loved my life in Los Angeles more, and we would never last. She was right. I went home, and a few weeks later, I asked your mother to marry me. I never saw Josie again."

"But you bought the building she was living in."

"I did. It came up for sale, and I didn't want to see her lose her home because she'd finally found her happy place after a harrowing year, and I wanted her to be happy. After I bought it, I had an associate ask her if she would be the manager."

"Did she know you were the owner?"

"She did. She told Steve she would love the job as long as she could work directly with him, and he had been instructed to say that was what was going to happen."

"And you never talked to her in thirty-five years?"

"Not until the week before you went there. I told her that my son needed to see a different life to make sure he knew what he really wanted. Four weeks had been just the right amount of time for me. I thought it would be for you as well."

He stared at his father. "Do you think you made the wrong choice in going home and marrying Mom?"

His dad didn't answer right away, then said, "Sometimes, I do."

Even though he'd known for most of his life that his parents weren't that in love with each other, he was still surprised to hear his dad admit that. "If you were unhappy, you could have gotten a divorce. You could have gone back to Ocean Shores and been with Josie."

"No, I couldn't. We'd said our goodbyes. And I didn't want to disrupt her life."

Everything finally clicked into place. "You don't want me to sell Ocean Shores because of Josie. Why didn't you just say that? Why the charade? The promise to live there for four weeks?" He felt a burst of anger. "Did you just want to mess with my life?"

"No," his father said sharply. "And I told you I would give you the choice to sell it or not. I just wanted you to go there. I wanted you to have time away from all this so you could make the best decision for what you wanted to do in your life."

"If I sell the property, then Josie ends up homeless. I can't believe that doesn't bother you. It's why you hung on to it all these years, isn't it?"

"Yes, but if you want to sell, we'll make sure that the tenants have enough money to go wherever they want to go. The amount of money we would make off the deal would more than cover that."

"Did Josie beg you not to sell when you talked to her?"

"No. She said things would work out the way they were meant to, and she would always be grateful for the past thirty-five years."

"That sounds like her," he said with a sigh. "But I still don't get your reasoning."

"I'm going to release you from the agreement," his father

said. "You can make the decision right now as to what you want to do. It's your call, Grayson. But before you tell me your answer, I want to know something: Did you have fun while you were there? Did you learn anything about yourself?"

He hated to give his father the satisfaction of being right, but he had no choice. "Yes. I had a great time, and I learned a lot about myself, about what I want."

"Which is what?"

"I've always wanted you to feel like I was a worthy successor, that you would be proud to turn your company over to me."

"I do feel that way, Grayson."

"I'm glad. But I can't run the company the way you did. I'm not you. And there will be changes going forward because I don't want to live a life that isn't authentically mine. I don't want to ever feel trapped in a web of my own making, which is basically the way you've described your life to me."

His father smiled. "That is a good description. I don't want you to get me wrong. I did love your mother. We had a lot in common. We had shared goals. And we wanted the same things."

"But you didn't have the magic with her that you felt with Josie." He paused. "Did you give Josie a locket?"

"I did. How did you know that?"

"Because Lexie and I found it in the cave, and Josie said she'd lost it a long time ago. You were there with her, weren't you? Did you and Josie scratch your initials into a heart on the wall of that cave, too?"

His father's gaze widened as he gave a nod. "Yes. We were in the cave and scratched our initials into the rocks. I can't believe they're still there."

"They are."

"Amazing." He let out a sigh. "When we got out of the cave, we stood on the rocks and watched the tide come in, and it felt like the water was erasing everything that had happened between us. Our time was up, literally and metaphorically. We kissed goodbye and I never saw her again."

"Did Mom know about Josie?"

"No. She never asked about my four weeks in Oceanside. Once I got back, she just pretended it had never happened, and so did I."

"How could you get married, knowing you cared about someone else?"

"Because Josie was right; she couldn't give me what I needed, and I knew that your mother and I were better suited."

"Were you?" he queried. "You've been separated for the last two decades, maybe not officially, but still..."

"Even if your mother and I weren't the perfect couple, I wouldn't have liked Josie's lifestyle. She wouldn't have been the right person for me, either, because I wanted a much bigger life than she did."

"That's true. I can't see you living at Ocean Shores."

"It would not have suited me, but it suited her, and I cared about her."

That actually made sense. "So you left the woman who filled you with passion for a woman whose ambitions matched your own. But you weren't all that happy with her, either. Why didn't you and Mom get divorced? Why stay together all these years?"

"I've never wanted to marry anyone else, and your mother has never wanted a divorce. We live our lives in a way that you don't understand, but it works for us."

"I don't understand it. I wouldn't want to be married to someone I didn't passionately love. But if it works for you and Mom, I guess I have no right to judge."

"I know we didn't provide the best example for a happy marriage. And I probably haven't provided the best example for running a large company, because I've been selfish, single-minded, and ruthlessly ambitious for most of my life."

"Which is why I can't understand why you wanted me to get to know the people I'm going to evict."

"Because I see you turning out like me, and I don't want that for you, Grayson. I can't tell you what to do. You have to live your own life, but I thought if I forced you to spend time in a place that had given me perspective, it might do the same for you." He paused. "You mentioned having had a few adventures while you were in Oceanside. Was there a woman involved in those trips?"

"Yes. Josie's niece, Lexie. She used to be a lawyer, but she gave that up to become a photographer. She's not as free-spirited as her aunt, but she has a creative passion that's inspiring. She looks at the world differently than I do. She's not about making money or having an important career. She's about telling a story, putting a light on something that no one has ever noticed before."

"Sounds like you care about her."

"I do, which is shocking because she has been the most vocal opponent of a possible building sale. She and Josie are the center of that community. And Lexie is a fighter. She is fiercely loyal to her friends, and she is stubborn as hell." He took a breath. "She will hate me forever if I sell the building. She loves it so much. They all do. Everyone who lives there. They welcomed me in even though I'm the enemy. Part of that was to try to charm me, but for the most part, they were genuine in their interactions with me."

"Which will make your decision more difficult."

"That's for sure."

"So, what's it going to be, Grayson?"

He gave his father a long look. "That property is worth millions to us. It could generate the most profit of anything we do this year."

"And if we don't sell, you'll make a lot of people very happy, one, in particular."

"Yes."

"It's not just about deciding whether or not you want to make this deal; it's about deciding who you want to be, what kind of life you want to lead. Go back to Ocean Shores, Grayson.

Figure out what you really want. And then you'll know what to do."

By Wednesday afternoon, Lexie was convinced that Grayson wasn't coming back to Ocean Shores. His car hadn't been seen in the lot, and his lights had been off since Saturday. He'd texted her on Monday to tell her that he was in LA, dealing with business and meeting with his father, and that he'd be in touch soon. That brief text had gotten her through Monday and Tuesday, but with no further word from him since then, her emotions had taken a dive, ranging from depression and sadness to irritation and anger.

She'd known that getting involved with him could lead her to this place, but she'd done it anyway. She'd flown past all the red flags, every barrier he'd thrown up, because she'd liked him so much. While it had started out as a fight for the building and for their community, it had turned into so much more.

But if it was over, it was over. And maybe it would be easier because her instincts were also telling her that he was drawing up the paperwork to sell the building and just didn't want to tell her that. Josie still hadn't lost faith, which was the only thing that kept her going. That and the contract she'd signed with *New Frontiers* magazine for a five-day trip to Morocco. One day of travel each way, and three days to complete her assignment. She'd be meeting up with a freelance writer while she was there and coordinating photos with him. And she could hardly believe that she would be leaving next Monday.

Her life might not be moving forward with Grayson, but it was moving forward, and she owed him something for that. His challenging attitude had been the kick-in-the-butt she'd needed to get moving on her dreams.

As she made her way through the empty courtyard to her apartment after finishing another shoot, she wondered how many more weeks she'd be making this walk. Hopefully, there would be a grace period of several months before she had to move.

She'd barely set down her things when a knock came at her door. She opened it, expecting to see her aunt, but it was Grayson, looking as handsome as ever, and her heart plummeted to her stomach. Not knowing what he was thinking had been terrible, but judging by his guarded expression, she wasn't sure getting answers from him would be any better.

"I thought you'd gone," she said.

"I told you I had to take care of some things in Los Angeles."

"That's what you said Monday morning. That was a long time ago."

"I know. Can I come in?"

She hesitated, then stepped back, waving him into her apartment. She shut the door behind him, not offering him a seat or a drink or anything. "Whatever you have to say, just say it. Because your silence has been driving me crazy, and I have to know what you're planning to do."

"I'm sorry. It hasn't been an easy decision. I needed to go back to LA, to my life, to remind myself of what my reality was."

"Right. Your stay at Ocean Shores was just an obligation," she said shortly.

"That's certainly the way I looked at it when I first got here, but it turned into a lot more than that. Getting to know Josie and the other tenants, and especially you, changed me in a way I never would have imagined. And it wasn't just that I started to think about this building differently, I began to think about myself differently, too."

Her heart was pounding against her chest. "Okay. But can you just tell me if you're selling or not? I can't stand the suspense another minute."

He gave her a long look, then said, "I'm not selling."

She couldn't hold back the tense breath she'd been holding. "You're serious? You're not selling? I didn't hear you wrong?"

"I'm not selling the building."

"I can't believe it. I was so sure you were going to make a different decision. What changed your mind?"

"You," he said, giving her a pointed look.

"Really?"

"How could I sell the thing you love the most?"

Her heart filled with emotion, and her eyes began to water. "Thank you. I know it probably wasn't the smartest business decision."

"It wasn't, but not all decisions should be about money. They should also be about people. And I like what you and Josie have built here. It's unique and special, and we could use more community and connection in the world, not less. I don't want to be the one to tear it down."

"I'm so glad, Grayson. I really thought this would go the other way."

"Like I said, it wasn't an easy decision because I've been focused on my career, my work, and nothing else since I graduated from college. Everything I have done has been to further those goals."

"I understand. Did you tell your father?"

"Yes."

"What did he say?"

A faint smile crossed his lips. "He was happy about it. But we didn't talk long because he had that 'I told you so' look in his eyes, and I didn't feel like hearing more about that."

She smiled back at him. "He said I told you so?"

"Basically. He sent me here to find myself, and he had a feeling that when I did that, I wouldn't want to sell. I hate to say he was right."

"But he was." She paused. "What happened with your other deal?"

"It fell through. I decided to stop trying to hold it together with desperate moves and let it go. There will be other opportunities. But this definitely hasn't been my most profitable month."

"You don't seem too upset about it."

"I'm not worried about the deals or the money anymore, but I do have one very pressing concern."

"What's that?"

"You," he said simply.

"What about me?" she asked carefully, her pulse beginning to race again at the gleam in his blue eyes.

"I like you, Lexie. Actually, that's not true. I'm falling in love with you, and I want you to be in my life." He moved closer, still leaving space between them as he gave her a questioning look. "I'm hoping you're feeling the same way."

"I am feeling the same way," she admitted. "Not talking to you the past five days almost killed me. I realized how much I want to talk to you and be with you."

A big smile spread across his face. "Thank God."

She laughed. "You weren't seriously worried, were you?"

"I was guardedly optimistic."

"That sounds like you. Guardedly...everything."

"That was the old me. The new me likes exploring dark caves and spooky national parks and watching you find new wonders in the world. Being here, being with you, made me realize I've been far too narrow-minded in my thinking, in my goals, in my life. I want to see more of the world and not because I'm making a deal, but because there's so much to see. And I want to see it with you."

"Speaking of seeing the world, I have something to tell you. I got a freelance job with *New Frontiers* magazine. They're sending me to Morocco for five days to do a shoot. And if I do a good job, there might be more work for me down the road, or, at least, I'll have a pipeline to sell whatever I do on my own."

"That's amazing, Lexie. How did that happen?"

"The editor is a friend of Sienna, who runs the Art Nest. Saying yes to that show has already opened more doors than I could have imagined. And it's because of you, Grayson. I had my big courageous moment when I quit the law firm, but then I backed off. I chose safety and security over what I quit for, which was to live my life in a more passionate, creative, imaginative way. And when you drove me to that wedding almost a month ago and asked me with your very specific brand of sarcastic cynicism whether I hadn't traded one form of servitude for another, I realized you were right. That's exactly what I'd done." She turned, pointing her hand to the dining room wall. "Notice anything different?"

He walked around her to take a closer look. "These are all your photos, and they're amazing. Just spectacular," he murmured, his gaze taking in each and every picture. Finally, he turned back around. "You got rid of all the other photos."

"I'm betting on myself now. I'm not going to live other people's dreams. I'm going to live my own." She smiled. "We turned out to be pretty good for each other, Grayson."

"Damn good," he said, walking back to her. "When are you going to Morocco?"

"Monday. When are you going back to LA?"

"Definitely not before Monday." He put his hands on her hips as he gazed into her eyes. "I want to spend as much time with you as I can."

"How are we going to do this, Grayson? I want to travel, not just to Morocco, to other places, too. I'll have to pick up some work for money in between, just to keep things going, but I feel like I'm going to be on the move for the next year or two. And I know you have a big job, a lot of responsibility. Can we make something between us work?"

"Absolutely," he said.

"I do like your confidence." She licked her lips. "I have to ask you something, though. Now that I've said I may not be spending much time here going forward, does that change how you feel about selling the building?"

"No," he said without a trace of doubt in his voice. "Because this is Josie's home. And Frank doesn't want to move again. I think he and Margaret might have something going on."

"I think that, too, but they're very cagey about it."

"Brad and Serena just had a baby. Kaia still needs to find the right guy. Emmalyn and Hunter need to be close to Bree and Olivia; Paige and Henry do as well. And Ava and Liam need to help Brad and Serena with the baby." He shrugged. "There are a lot of connections here."

She smiled. "I can't believe you just went through so many names without even a pause. You're part of this community now."

"What do you say we make Ocean Shores our home base for the next year? We figure out our work and travel schedules from there. Maybe we take some trips together. I can look for real estate to develop. You can look for the perfect photo shoot locations."

"But you're a rich guy. Do you really want to live in your apartment or in mine?"

"I don't care where we live, as long as we're together. I was being too guarded when I said before that I was falling in love with you. The truth is: I'm already there. I know it's fast and completely out of character for me, but it's how I feel. When I drove back to LA, I thought I might feel differently being farther away from you, but it was worse. I missed you every second of every day. And nothing seemed as important as getting back to you." He paused, looking deep into her eyes. "You inspire me, Lexie. You make me want to be a better version of myself. And I want to do the same for you."

She wrapped her arms around his neck, feeling the last of her worries slipping away. "I love you, too, Grayson. And you have inspired me to cancel a bunch of jobs and fly off to Morocco, so I think you've already done a lot."

"I'm really proud of you, Lexie."

"I'm proud of me, too. And I hope I can help you find a deal that will be even better than selling this building, because I want everyone to win."

"You know that rarely happens."

"Well, it's happening right now, so I'll take it. Now, are you going to kiss me or what?"

"I'm going to kiss you, and later, much later, I'm going to tell you about my father and Josie."

"Wait! What?"

"Later," he said as he captured her mouth and gave her a kiss filled with emotion and promise for the future.

And she didn't want to think or talk anymore, either. But later...

CHAPTER NINETEEN

It was Thursday morning before they got to *later*. After the second-best night of his life, the first also being with her, he brought Lexie coffee in bed. Then he slid under the covers next to her to fulfill the promise he'd made the night before.

"So, tell me about Josie and your dad," Lexie said as she sipped her coffee. "And by the way, this is really good. This is not my coffee, is it?"

"I went back to my apartment and grabbed mine," he said with a smile as he sipped from the mug he'd brought for himself.

"Did you run into anyone?"

"No."

"I can't wait to tell everyone they don't have to move. I feel a little guilty that I didn't do it last night, but you were just too distracting..."

"I think that was you," he said with a laugh, feeling so relaxed and happy he was almost afraid it was too good to be true.

"It was us," she said. "Okay, tell me the story."

He set his mug on the nightstand. "My dad was here on a business trip thirty-five years ago. He met Josie on a beach and thought she was beautiful, fiery, and passionate. She told him she'd just left her husband and her career in Hollywood to find herself, to be who she was supposed to be, no more pretending, no more acting."

"That's what she told me."

"It made a big impression on my father. He was about to get engaged to the woman who would be my mother, and he was building his business, a business that he would merge with her family's company, and he was feeling stressed and not sure if he was on the right path. For a few weeks, they played in the ocean, explored the caves—"

Her eyes widened. "Oh, my God. He gave her the necklace, didn't he?"

"He did. And that heart you photographed with the blurry initials. They were their initials. It was the last day they were together. When they stood on the rocks watching the tide come in, he said he felt like the ocean was washing away everything that they'd had. It was where they shared their last kiss."

"And where we shared our first," she murmured, meeting his gaze. "That's oddly symmetrical."

"I agree." He paused. "Anyway, at first I thought he'd been the one to leave Josie, but she was the one who told him to go home, that his life was elsewhere. So, he went back to LA and married my mother and merged his company with her family's company, and the rest is history."

"That's a crazy story. Did your father already own this building when he met Josie?"

"No. He bought it for her. He wanted her to be able to always live in the place she'd come to love. He said she knew he was the owner when she became the manager, and she only agreed if she could deal solely with his representative, which she did." He could see the puzzled gleam in her eyes and knew what question was coming. "You want to know if my father wanted to sell. He never did. But when he was thinking about retirement, and we were going over all the company holdings, I pushed him to move the building into my control. We had a lot of arguments about it over the past two years. I didn't understand why he didn't want to sell, and he wouldn't explain."

"Maybe because he didn't want to tell you he'd loved someone else besides your mother right before he got engaged."

"That was probably part of it. He definitely got annoyed with me asking to sell, and he kept saying I wasn't looking at the bigger picture. I didn't know what the hell that meant because I was focused on making money for the company I was going to take over. Apparently, he decided I was too much like him, and maybe I needed to experience the Ocean Shores magic for myself to see if it would change my mind. He wanted to force me to take a break, to step outside of my world, my bubble, and see what else was out there. And he thought meeting Josie would be good for me." He paused. "He said he spoke to her the week before I came. He didn't say what they discussed, but it was the first time they'd communicated in thirty-five years."

"And that's why Aunt Josie was never as worried as I was about the building being sold. She was convinced that being here would change your mind."

"As you were," he reminded her.

"I wasn't convinced at all," she denied. "I knew it would be nearly impossible to change your mind."

"But you did," he said with a smile. "And being here at Ocean Shores did change my perspective. I was caught up in a world of money and deals and ruthless ambition. I didn't have real friends; I had associates. The women I've dated shared the same sort of ambition in a different way. They wanted to marry someone like me. They wanted to live in the same world I wanted to live in, but they didn't have their own goals, their own passions. I never wanted to be with someone who just wanted to be an extension of me."

"Well, I'm definitely not that."

"No, you're not. And I'm not the way I was a month ago. I've changed. I've seen another world, one that I would prefer to live in."

"But you're still you, Grayson. It's okay to be driven, to want to build a company, to want to develop real estate. You have a lot of power and money to change lives. You just have to use it for good."

"I never thought I was using it for evil," he said with a laugh. "But I wasn't taking into consideration the fact that there are always people behind the numbers. I hope to be a realistic but also compassionate businessman going forward. And I'm hoping you'll keep me on track."

"I won't need to," she said confidently. "Because you are a good man."

"Thank you."

"Now, getting back to your father's story, did your dad think he made the right choice?"

"Yes."

"But you said your parents barely live together, right?"

"Right. They've been living separately for a long time. Apparently, that's the way they like it. I don't understand their marriage, but I know I don't want that kind of relationship for myself."

"I don't either. When I'm in, I go all in. No half measures for me. And if you ever feel you can't be all in, too, then we call this thing off. We have the hard conversation, because if we can't tell each other the truth, then what are we doing?"

He loved the fervor in her voice, the passion in her gaze. "I'll always tell you the truth, even if it's difficult. I never lied to you about my intentions."

"No, you didn't, and that's why I trust you. Why I love you."

"I love you, too."

She set down her coffee and kissed him.

He loved the sweet taste of her mouth, flavored from the Italian roast she'd just consumed. He also loved the way her hands moved across his body, the way she helped him off with his shirt, the way they made love to each other again, sealing the promise they'd just made to each other.

Four days later, on Sunday night, Lexie finished packing her suitcase under the careful watch of Kaia and Emmalyn.

"I can't believe you're leaving," Kaia said.

"Did you pack the travel sized, plug-in carbon monoxide detector I gave you?" Emmalyn asked.

She smiled at Emmalyn's worried expression. "It's in my carry-on. But I'm staying in a hotel."

"Stop trying to make her nervous, Em," Kaia interrupted. "You'll be fine, Lexie."

"I know, and Emmalyn isn't making me nervous because I'm already nervous."

"I know you'll have a great time," Emmalyn said. "I can't wait to see the photos you bring back."

"I just hope I can live up to everyone's expectations. If I do well, this could be the beginning of my second career."

"You'll do great," Kaia assured her. "You're so talented, Lexie. Now the rest of the world will see it." She paused. "How come Grayson isn't helping you pack? You two have been inseparable since he decided not to sell the building."

"He went with Frank to talk to a potential buyer for the Mustang. He's very invested in Frank and that car."

"Your plan worked. We just had to make him like us," Emmalyn said with a smile. "Then he wouldn't be able to sell our homes."

"I think it's Lexie who made that happen," Kaia said with a teasing smile. "She decided to really make him like her."

"It was a tough job, but someone had to do it," she snapped back with a grin.

"So tough," Kaia said. "Having to fall in love with a smart, successful, attractive man. What a sacrifice."

"I didn't even think I could like him a little when he first got here, but he wasn't who I thought he was. He was much, much better. And he really pushed me to do more with my life, which is why I'm going to Morocco." She zipped her suitcase and put it on the floor. "Let's go see if we can help with the barbecue."

"It's not just a barbecue; it's a party," Kaia said. "We're going to say 'Bon Voyage' to you and 'Welcome Home' to Grayson."

"Grayson will appreciate that. He probably still feels a little like an outsider."

"He's not an outsider; he's our hero," Emmalyn said.

"Who's your hero?" Grayson asked from the doorway.

She caught her breath at the sight of him, wondering if it would always be like that when they saw each other after being apart, if only for a few hours. "Em is talking about you."

"You saved the building," Emmalyn said. "We're all really grateful."

"You did save the building, but you were also the one to put it at risk," Kaia interjected, always the one to inject some realism into the conversation. "So, I'm not sure I'd call you a hero, Grayson, but I will say thank you."

"You're welcome," Grayson said. "And you're right, I'm not a hero, but I hope to be a good fellow tenant."

"Don't get carried away with that tenant nonsense; you're still the owner," Kaia said.

He grinned. "That is true. But we all know Josie is in charge, and that's not going to change."

"You did turn out to be a decent guy," Kaia said. "Which I'm happy about. Because I want only the best for my friend."

"I want the best for her, too," he said, his gaze meeting hers.

"Why don't we meet you outside?" Kaia said, urging Emmalyn out of the room.

Grayson walked toward her as they left. "Are you all packed?"

"Yes, and the nerves are getting stronger."

"It's good to be nervous. That means you're doing something exciting."

"I'll try to hang on to that thought. What happened with Frank's car?"

"He sold it for twice the amount he was thinking."

"Was that because of you? Did you negotiate for him?"

"I might have had some input," he conceded. Taking a breath, he said, "I'm already starting to miss you."

"I'm not leaving until tomorrow morning."

"I know. But it's how I feel."

"It's how I feel, too. I can't believe the timing of all this. I fall in love with you, and then my career suddenly catches a tailwind, and I'm flying away from you."

"You're not flying away from me. You're flying toward your future, and I will be here when you come back."

"I like the sound of that. Everyone keeps asking me if you really want to live here. We could get a house nearby, a place with a big home office, maybe a view of the water. Our lives don't have to be here."

"We'll figure it out. Let's not worry about anything now."

"Okay," she said, sliding her arms around his waist. "I love that I can kiss you whenever I want to."

He smiled. "Then what are you waiting for?"

She gave him a kiss, savoring the taste of his mouth, the heat of their embrace, the certainty that he was absolutely the right man for her. But after a minute, she forced herself to pull away.

"We were just getting started," he protested.

"We have a party to get to." She took his hand and led him out of her apartment. Before they could get to the pool area, they ran into Josie, who gave them both a hug.

"It makes my heart so happy to see you two together," she said, her warm gaze encompassing both of them. "Grayson, you've done a wonderful thing keeping this community intact. And, Lexie, I don't believe any of this would have happened without you. So, I want to thank you both. I love this place, but I love the people even more, especially you two."

"We love you, too," she said.

Josie's gaze moved to Grayson. "I'm very glad your father sent you here."

"He knew what I needed. Just as you knew what he needed when you sent him home thirty-five years ago."

She nodded. "Yes. He needed someone who wasn't me. But I cared about him a great deal, and I was always thankful for him giving me a home all these years. He didn't have to do that." She paused. "Let's join the party. Everyone wants to celebrate both of you."

As they moved into the courtyard, Lexie looked around at all of her friends, feeling blessed to have this incredible support group. They hugged and thanked Grayson, who awkwardly accepted the accolades coming his way. He wasn't a man who liked to be the center of attention, but he was tonight.

As the party went on, they ate, drank, talked, and laughed until it grew late in the evening, and they finally made their way back to her apartment.

Grayson shut the door behind them and gave her a smile. "That was a great night."

She grabbed his hand. "It's going to get even better. I love you, Grayson. It's amazing how we started out as enemies and turned into lovers. I don't know exactly when that happened."

"It happened when I saw you in the hot pink bikini the first night I arrived," he said with a sexy smile.

"No way. You hated me then."

"I hated that I didn't," he corrected. "And I'm blaming that on the bikini."

She smiled. "I had no idea. I thought it was Henry's ball that distracted you and sent you flailing into the pool."

He grinned back at her. "That was part of it. But you were the other part."

"I'm so happy, Grayson. I almost wish I wasn't leaving tomorrow."

He shook his head. "I don't want you to wish that. I'm

excited for you, and I can't wait to hear all about it. You're going to be great. This is what you were meant to do, Lexie."

"Thanks for believing in me."

"Thanks for showing me a life I couldn't imagine before I came here."

"A life that's just getting started," she said as she led him into the bedroom.

WHAT TO READ NEXT...

Are you excited to go back to Ocean Shores?
Don't miss the next book in the series,

Love Me Like You Do

Have you missed any of the Ocean Shores Books?

Ocean Shores Series

Hopelessly Romantic

Summer Loving

Moonlight Feels Right

Blame It On The Bikini

Love Me Like You Do

For a complete list of books, visit www.barbarafreethy.com

ABOUT THE AUTHOR

Barbara Freethy is a #1 New York Times Bestselling Author of 95 novels ranging from contemporary romance to romantic suspense and women's fiction. With over 13 million copies sold, thirty-three of Barbara's books have appeared on the New York Times and USA Today Bestseller Lists, including SUMMER SECRETS which hit #1 on the New York Times!

Known for her emotional and compelling stories of love, family, mystery and romance, Barbara enjoys writing about ordinary people caught up in extraordinary adventures. Library Journal says, "Freethy has a gift for creating unforgettable characters."

For additional information, please visit Barbara's website at www.barbarafreethy.com.

Made in the USA
Middletown, DE
25 September 2025